That was when Jade got her first look at the next rider. It was Sloan. She hadn't seen him in more than two days, and she was hungry to get her fill. Dressed in leather chaps and vest, he looked the part of man in charge. He strolled up to the powerful animal and stroked him. There was a gentleness to his touch she could see even from far away.

Neighing, the horse danced away, but two ranch hands held him steady as Sloan checked the cinch.

"Whoa, fella." He coaxed him back in a low, steady voice. Knight blew out a breath, as if saying he didn't trust him.

Jade couldn't take her eyes off the man or the animal. Pushing his black hat down on his head, Sloan approached the horse. Reins in hand, he grabbed the saddle horn. Then he raised his booted foot in the stirrup and climbed on just as the horse swung around in a circle. Gripping the reins, he pulled them back as the animal reared.

Sloan was ready.

Knight bucked, and then bucked again. Power against power, stubbornness against stubbornness, the dance continued on for what seemed an endless amount of time. Neither willing to give in.

It was incredible to watch.

Dear Readers

This is my second book in *The Quilt Shop in Kerry Springs* series, and I hope you are enjoying the citizens of the small Texas town as much as I do writing about them.

In THE LONESOME RANCHER I'm back out at the ranch with the Merrick family. Besides their being a Texas ranching dynasty, there's been a Merrick in the US Congress for the past three generations. Yet my hero, Sloan Merrick, the adopted son of Clay and Louisa, has no desire to leave the ranch.

My heroine, Jade Hamilton, comes to the ranch in hopes of finding her biological father. Not for the fame or fortune that comes with the Merrick name, but to learn where she comes from. And, of course, what we all want: love. Just to feel a sense of belonging.

Jade tries to tell herself that once she meets her father, Clay Merrick, she can walk away. What she doesn't realise is how much the family will come to mean to her—especially Sloan. If he learns the truth, will she lose him too?

Coming from such a large family, I know how lucky I am to have so many who love and care about me. I can't imagine what it's like when you learn you're not who you think you are.

Of course I'll give Sloan and Jade their happy ending, but their journey will be an interesting one. Hope you enjoy the ride.

Patricia Thayer

THE LONESOME RANCHER

BY
PATRICIA THAYER

First published in Great Britain 2011
by Mills & Boon, an imprint of Harlequin (UK) Limited,
Eton House, 18-24 Paradise Road, Richmond, Surrey TW9 1SR

© Patricia Wright 2011

ISBN: 978 0 263 22102 2

Harlequin (UK) policy is to use papers that are natural, renewable
and recyclable products and made from wood grown in sustainable
forests. The logging and manufacturing process conform to the
legal environmental regulations of the country of origin.

Printed and bound in Great Britain
by CPI Antony Rowe, Chippenham, Wiltshire

Originally born and raised in Muncie, Indiana, **Patricia Thayer** is the second of eight children. She attended Ball State University, and soon afterwards headed West. Over the years she's made frequent visits back to the Midwest, trying to keep up with her growing family.

Patricia has called Orange County, California, home for many years. She not only enjoys the warm climate, but also the company and support of other published authors in the local writers' organisation. For the past eighteen years she has had the unwavering support and encouragement of her critique group. It's a sisterhood like no other.

When she's not working on a story, you might find her travelling the United States and Europe, taking in the scenery and doing story research while thoroughly enjoying herself accompanied by Steve, her husband for over thirty-five years. Together they have three grown sons and four grandsons. As she calls them, her own true-life heroes. On rare days off from writing, you might catch her at Disneyland, spoiling those grandkids rotten! She also volunteers for the Grandparent Autism Network.

Patricia has written for over twenty years, and has authored over thirty-six books for Silhouette and Harlequin Mills & Boon. She has been nominated for both the National Readers' Choice Award and the prestigious RITA. Her book NOTHING SHORT OF A MIRACLE won a *RT Book Reviews* Reviewer's Choice award.

A long-time member of Romance Writers of America, she has served as President and held many other board positions for her local chapter in Orange County. She's a firm believer in giving back.

Check her website at www.patriciathayer.com for upcoming books.

To my mother. You're my hero.

PROLOGUE

BREAKING NEWS

SENATOR CLAYTON MERRICK rushed home to Texas to be at his wife's bedside after she suffered a stroke. A family spokesperson reports that Louisa Merrick is resting comfortably.

Will this serious medical crisis mean this is the last term for the U.S. senator? More importantly, how does this affect the upcoming vote on the pending energy bill...and the Merrick political dynasty?

CHAPTER ONE

JADE HAMILTON was totally lost, in more ways than she could count.

She pulled to the curb and parked her compact car on Main Street in Kerry Springs, Texas. The traffic was nearly nonexistent. Well, what did she expect? The population was under twenty thousand. Talk about your small town. Of course she knew that when she'd done her research on the area.

She blew out a breath. This was one of those crossroad moments…her friend, fellow nurse, Carrie Bradley, had always talked about. Either she needed to get directions to the job interview, or forget this crazy idea and turn around and head back to Dallas.

Then she'd never learn the truth. She had to know the truth.

Sadness crept over her, thinking about the past few months. Jade hated the resentment she felt for the woman who'd raised her, yet they'd kept so many secrets. Now Renee Hamilton was gone and she couldn't tell Jade anything. Anything about the information Jade had found in the safe-deposit box that would change her life forever.

It was time she find out the entire truth. For her own

satisfaction she needed answers. First, she had to find River's End Ranch.

With renewed determination, she climbed out of the car and looked along the street to see a hardware store, a drugstore and ice cream store. Then a storefront with a display of handmade quilts caught her eye. The name Blind Stitch Quilt Shop was embossed across the glass window. She smiled, remembering her childhood and the hours she'd spent learning how to stitch with her mother.

Jade walked to the entrance, opened the door as a bell rang overhead. Inside the cool air mingled with the chatter of several women gathered around a cutting table. The salesclerk seemed to be busy so, having plenty of time before her appointment, Jade took the opportunity to look around the quaint shop. Several beautiful quilts adorned the high walls, underneath were stacks of pattern books and displays of scissors, needles and other notices. She strolled through the bolts of colorful fabric into a connecting room where another group of ladies were gathered around a table. She was surprised to see there was a man who was the center of attention.

Jade enjoyed a leisurely gaze over the handsome guy. He held his Stetson in his hand so she could see his inky-black hair and dark, deep-set eyes. She recognized more than a hint of Hispanic heritage in his strong jawline.

He was dressed in a starched cream-colored Western shirt, and new-looking pair of jeans, but he had on boots that were well-worn. She glanced down at his hands, and could see blunt-cut nails, also the callused fingers. He was definitely a working cowboy.

In a quilt shop?

"He's pretty easy on the eyes, huh?"

Jade swung around and found a pretty blonde about her age, smiling at her.

"I'm sorry," Jade admitted. "It's rude to stare."

"It's hard not to," the woman said. "There are some good-looking men around Kerry Springs. I can say that since I've recently married the most handsome one, Evan Rafferty. Hi, I'm Jenny Rafferty."

"Jade Hamilton," she said, smiling.

"Welcome, Jade, to the Blind Stitch. What can I do for you? Sign you up for my quilting class, or..." She grinned, and then said, "Maybe introduce you to that good-looking cowboy."

Jade shook her head. She couldn't get distracted from her goal. "Oh, no. I'm sorry, but I only came in to get directions."

"So are you looking for a place to live?"

Jade found herself relaxing a little. "A job first."

Jenny laughed. "That's always a good idea. Where are you headed? I'm fairly new to the community, but I can give pretty good directions."

"I'm looking for Louisa Merrick at the River's End Ranch."

The store clerk raised an eyebrow. "Really? Louisa is one of our best patrons...until recently."

"So you know where the ranch is?"

"Yes, I do." She nodded to the cowboy. "But I think he can do a better job of giving directions. That's Louisa's son, Sloan Merrick."

Jade saw the man had started for the door carrying one of the sample books. "Okay, thank you, Jenny," she called as she hurried across the room, hoping she could follow him out to the ranch.

He'd just gotten out the door when she called to him. "Excuse me, Mr. Merrick."

The man was at his truck. He turned around and was even more handsome close up, and much bigger.

He frowned as he gave her the once-over, causing a funny reaction in her stomach.

He straightened. "What do you want?"

"Huh, well…" She was suddenly nervous. "Jenny Rafferty told me that you're Sloan Merrick. I was wondering if I could get directions to the River's End." She forced a smile. "I have an appointment with Louisa Merrick."

He continued to stare, but his eyes narrowed sharply. "The only directions you'll get from me are to tell you how to leave town."

She blinked. "I beg your pardon."

He stepped closer. "How much plainer do you need it, lady? Stay the hell away from Merrick land, you aren't welcome."

An hour later, Jade had found her way out to the ranch. She was still fighting the urge to turn and run as she looked past the high wrought-iron gate toward the huge white house perched on the hill.

Her gaze moved to the miles of split-rail fencing enclosing the many acres of green pastures where Hereford steers grazed on the large southern Texas cattle ranch. She looked up at the archway overhead that read River's End, owned by the Merrick Family, est. 1904.

She blew out a breath to slow her heart rate. It didn't help. Go back to Dallas and forget she'd ever heard the name Merrick. At least one Merrick doesn't want you here.

There was still time to change her mind, to forget this crazy idea. Then she'd never learn the truth about herself.

She pushed the button on the intercom. "Merrick residence," a woman with a heavy accent answered.

Jade swallowed the dryness in her throat. "Hello, I'm Jade Hamilton. I have an appointment with Mrs. Merrick." Her heart pounded hard in her chest. Was she finally going to meet the senator?

"I'll open the gate for you. Drive to the main house."

Jade climbed back into her car and the gate swung open as Sloan Merrick's threat echoed in her head.

"Stay the hell away from Merrick land. You aren't welcome." Maybe she would be, or maybe she wouldn't be, but this was her chance to find out the truth.

She drove through the gate and tried to enjoy the quarter mile trip as she continued along the road and passed several structures, including a large barn and a corral with a number of horses. There were ranch hands busy with chores. A few of them looked at her, but no one stopped her so she kept on going.

The house was more impressive the closer she got. The brick and white clapboard, three-story structure with a big wraparound porch was loaded down with huge pots of flowers adding a rainbow of color. She pulled into the circular driveway.

Grabbing her purse and briefcase she headed up the slate tile walkway to the steps and a massive oak door with a cut-glass window. The name Merrick was etched into the center.

Each breath Jade drew was more labored. She'd

waited months to come here, to meet the one man linked to the secret of her past. She couldn't lose her nerve.

Sloan Merrick studied his mother seated on the sofa in the sunroom. Even being in her favorite place in the house, she didn't look happy. She'd turned fifty-eight on her last birthday, but the past few months had taken a toll on her.

Since her stroke Louisa Merrick hadn't cared much about her appearance. Her hair hadn't been cut or styled, and even the manicurist had been turned away when she'd come by the house. It was so unlike Mother not to want to see anyone, not friends or family. Even though the doctor felt she could make a full recovery with exercise and therapy, she hadn't put forth much effort. And Sloan was worried about her.

"The women at the shop send their best wishes. Liz, Beth, Millie and Jenny all asked about you."

She looked at him, and then down at items he'd brought her back from The Blind Stitch.

"Liz thought you'd like the new pattern book. She told me to tell you that they hadn't started the quilt yet. They need your help on colors and design."

"That's about all I could do. I'd be useless to them the way I am now."

"That could change," he said, hoping to get a rise out of her.

Bingo. She glared at him. "I know your intentions are good, son. But I'm handling this."

But she wasn't handling it. "Mother, if you'll just let us help you…"

"That's the problem, Sloan. Everyone is always helping me. It's time I start doing things on my own."

She waved her good arm. "Or I might as well be an invalid."

He could see her frustration. Hell, he had a big share of his own. Her strong Spanish heritage showed in her distinctive bone structure and coloring, especially her deep brown eyes.

"I know how important your independence is to you."

"Then get ready because I'm planning on getting it back. And soon."

He stared at her, recalling the day she'd collapsed in front of him. Thank God she'd gotten immediate medical attention. And as the wife of a U.S. senator, she'd had the best care. "You haven't gotten all your strength back. There are times when you need someone to help you."

"I agree. That's why I'm planning on hiring someone to help me get back on my feet."

"What? Why didn't you say something? If you needed help we're here."

She shook her head. "No, you, your father and Alisa need to get on with your lives. I want—no, need—to do this on my own. Thankfully I still have my faculties. My mind isn't completely gone. That's why I'm hiring a nurse to be with me until I'm back on solid ground, so to speak."

Sloan calmed down a little. Okay, maybe that wasn't such a bad idea. Marta had been overworked with the housework and Mother's demands. "So who did the doctor recommend?"

"He gave me the name of a nurses' registry that specializes in this sort of thing. I've been interviewing several candidates and I found one I like."

Before Sloan could speak there was a knock on the

door and the longtime housekeeper, Marta, peered in. "*Señorita* Hamilton is here."

Louisa smiled. "Good. Send her in, Marta." Then she glanced at him. "Don't you have somewhere to be?"

He folded his arms across his chest, leaned a hip against the desk and looked toward the doorway. "Not hardly."

When the candidate walked into the room, Sloan froze. The woman from town.

She was an attractive female with dark hair cut in a straight style that moved freely just below her chin. She glanced up at him and his breath caught. Those large eyes, a rich green and tilted upward at the corners, had thrown him off guard just an hour ago and were still having the same effect on him now.

He quickly recovered and stood. "You don't seem to take direction well, Ms. Hamilton."

"Maybe because it's Mrs. Merrick who wanted to see me. It seemed right that she should be the one to tell me to leave."

"Wrong," he told her. "Too many people like to take advantage. It's surprising how lucrative a story about the Merricks is, so I'm very protective of my family."

"Sloan. Please, at least let Ms. Hamilton catch her breath before you give her the third degree."

Jade Hamilton walked to the wicker sofa and sat down next to his mother. "Mrs. Merrick, it's so nice to finally meet you. You have a lovely home. It's so bright and sunny in here."

The sunroom had rows of windows that overlooked the rose garden. It also expressed his mother's culture with the hand-painted floor tiles and brightly colored walls.

Sloan saw Ms. Hamilton had turned a bright smile at his mother. "It must be a comfort to you to be able to be in familiar surroundings during your recovery."

"It is," Louisa said as her eyes brightened. "I decorated this house, turned it into a home right after Sloan and I moved in." She looked at him. "Remember, son, how the place resembled a museum?"

"Yes, Mother, I do."

"I had my husband add this room. I needed sunlight...and some color."

Sloan cleared his throat. "Maybe we should start the interview."

Ms. Hamilton blinked those gorgeous eyes at him. "I thought your mother already had." She turned back to Louisa. "What questions do you want to ask me, Mrs. Merrick?"

"I think it's time you call me Louisa."

"And I'm Jade."

"What a lovely name. I can see why your mother named you that. Your eyes are striking."

Jade couldn't stop shaking, afraid that any minute they'd discover who she was. "Thank you. My mother told me when she saw their color she couldn't come up with anything else."

Sloan stood. He wasn't going to be taken in by a pretty face again. Not where his mother was concerned.

"Around here we're big on family names," Louisa continued. "My son was christened John Sloan Merrick. Sloan is his biological father's name and then my husband, Clay, adopted him when he was eight."

Sloan crossed the room. "Mother, I don't think we need to go into family history."

"He's right," Jade said, giving him a sideways glance.

"This is an interview. Ask me whatever you want, Mr. Merrick."

"Your last place of employment?"

Jade reached into her oversize purse and pulled out her résumé. She handed it to him. "I worked at a small private hospital in Dallas before I took a leave of absence to be with my mother during the last months before she passed away." Jade felt the tears and willed them not to fall. "She had multiple sclerosis for years."

"Oh, I'm sorry." Louisa sighed. "That must have been so hard on you."

Jade didn't expect to feel an instant liking for this woman. That was what made this so hard. "Thank you. My consolation is that I know she's isn't suffering any longer."

"That has to be comforting for you," the older woman said as she took hold of her hand.

Jade saw the woman's honest concern and felt the warmth in her touch. She also had the sudden urge to run out and forget it all, especially with Sloan Merrick watching her so closely. She wanted this job. It would be her best chance to get to see the senator. "Enough about me. What about you, Louisa?"

Sloan started to speak, but his mother sent him a look. He backed off.

Louisa's expression softened as she said, "I want my life back. And I'll do whatever it takes."

Jade found herself smiling. "That's the good news. And as we discussed on the phone, I plan to help you do that. It will also take some hard work and determination on your part."

Louisa's son did interrupt this time. "Well, we want

to thank you for coming by, Ms. Hamilton. We will let you know our decision."

Jade rose from the sofa. Okay, so it wasn't a total success. He would get her out of there before she could meet any of the family, or allow Louisa to make a decision. "I'll be staying in town at the Cross Creek Bed and Breakfast for the next few days." She started for the French doors when she heard her name.

"Jade, wait," Louisa called to her.

She paused and turned around.

"There's no need to go yet," the older woman told her. "This is my decision."

"Mother," Sloan said, visibly unhappy.

The older woman straightened. "No, Sloan, this is my choice. Since this happened…" She held up her arm. "No one has asked me how I feel about anything. Well, I'm telling you how I feel now. I asked Jade to come here."

Jade spoke up, hoping to calm the situation. "It's okay, Louisa. Maybe your husband should be involved in this decision, too."

"Clay? He's busy working on an energy bill in Washington." She sighed. "Take some advice, Jade, don't get involved with a politician. They're never home, and your private life gets plastered all over the newspapers."

Jade stiffened. "I'll remember that."

Sloan wanted to be as enthusiastic as his mother. But years in the political circus had made him leery of strangers, especially when it came to his family's privacy. For himself, he'd been burned good, too, but managed to survive. Yet, he still didn't trust strangers. "Mother, I have some questions for Ms. Hamilton."

She frowned. "I'm not going to change my mind. This is my decision to make."

He knew he'd gotten his stubbornness from Louisa Cruz Sloan Merrick. The daughter of poor immigrants, she was a one-time beauty queen, and had worked hard to graduate college and marry well. Twice. And she'd been the best mother a son could ask for.

"Do you have any objection if I take Jade for a walk in the garden?"

His mother glared at him.

"I'm only going to warn her about how persistent you can be when you want your way."

Louisa turned to Jade and smiled sweetly. "Did I warn you how impossible my son could be?"

Jade smiled. "He's only concerned about you."

His mother turned back to him. "I will give you fifteen minutes. Then I'd like to show Jade the exercise room upstairs. That's where I'll be."

Marta came through the door and helped Louisa with her walker.

A distant cousin, Marta had worked for the family since she was a girl. Now both she and her husband, Miguel, were employed by the Merricks. Louisa had always been loyal to her family and friends.

Being too trusting was one of his mother's faults. That and being sucked in by strangers. Jade Hamilton was definitely a stranger. He'd learned the hard way that trouble sometimes comes wrapped in pretty packages. Crystal Erickson had been beautiful and distracting. So much so, he let his guard down. It had been an embarrassment for the family. Never again.

After his mother left, Sloan crossed the room and opened the doors that led onto a large patio area and the garden beyond.

"Let's take advantage of the pleasant fall weather."

Jade stepped out into the brick patio framed with large ceramic pots of flowers. A manicured lawn was edged with numerous tea roses of every imaginable color. "Oh, my, this is lovely."

"Gardening is another of my mother's many hobbies. She loves to quilt, too."

"It's nice that she has so many interests."

"That she does. She's always been active."

"Good. Then she'll want to get involved in her life again."

Sloan eyed the attractive woman. She stood about five-seven, with long legs encased in tailored navy slacks and a simple white blouse tucked into her narrow waist. Very businesslike, but he was still curious as to why she'd come all this way for a job.

"Okay, let's cut to the chase, Ms. Hamilton. Why are you really here?"

CHAPTER TWO

JADE willed herself to relax. He couldn't know the real reason.

"I don't understand, Mr. Merrick. I've explained that my mother passed away recently."

"Dallas is about six hundred miles from Kerry Springs."

She arched an eyebrow. "And that sends up a red flag to you?"

"Several. Having a father who's a U.S. senator will do that to you."

"I didn't ask specifically for this area, but when I decided to return to work, I signed on with a nurses' registry. This position came up and I decided a different area might be a nice change."

She met his gaze, refusing to be intimidated. "I must have checked out, or your mother would never have set up an interview. And she seems to approve of me." Jade paused for a few erratic heartbeats. "I thought I was here to help *her?*"

She looked over the handsome man. Tall and well-built, he had Louisa's large brown eyes. She had yet to see his smile.

"Of course," he told her. "And I'm here to protect her."

"The loyal son."

He shrugged. "You took care of your mother, I'm sure she had your loyalty, too."

With a nod, Jade glanced away. There were a lot of memories both good and bad, and some she'd like to forget. Now she needed to find out who she was.

"No siblings, no father in Dallas?"

"No siblings. No father," she repeated. "It's all in my résumé." She wasn't going to beg this man for a job, no matter how much she wanted to meet Clay Merrick. "I think it's time we end this, and you can discuss your dislikes with your mother after she finishes interviewing me. Thank you for your time."

She headed toward the house, praying that he would call her back, but he didn't. Okay, so this wasn't going to work out. Then he finally spoke her name.

"Ms. Hamilton," he called as she reached the doorway.

Her heart was pounding hard against the ribs as she turned and waited. "Yes?"

"Okay, if my mother gives you the position, I'll agree to a week trial period."

"You'll agree? I thought it was your mother's choice? After all she brought me here."

"And I have to protect my family."

She was frustrated. "I have excellent references, Mr. Merrick. I'm highly qualified for this position. A position that isn't even permanent. Just admit it, you don't want me here."

Sloan looked uncomfortable. "I didn't say that. I'd put anyone on a trial basis." He glared at her. "And whether I like it or not, I am a product of my father's very public profession. Sometimes it's hard for me to trust people. But my mother trusts you and that's what's

important. So if she gives you the job, I won't interfere."

Guilt washed over her. She'd got what she wanted.
All she'd been looking for was a small piece of this life,
this family.

An hour later, Jade had been hired as Louisa's nurse,
and shown the equipment that would rival some hospi-
tals' therapy rooms.

Now, she was standing outside what would be her
living quarters for the next month or so. She'd gotten
the job, but she didn't feel like she expected to feel. For
the first time since learning of Clay Merrick, she was
questioning her decision to come here.

She opened the door and her breath caught. It was not
where she expected to stay, not as hired staff. There was
a sitting room with the walls painted a buttery-yellow,
and carpet a light shade of green. A love seat was covered in ivory chenille and faced a marble fireplace. All
the furniture looked to be expensive antiques.

She continued through double doors and saw a
four-poster bed with a sheer canopy draping over the
top. The bedspread was a hand-sewn quilt in yellow
and green hues. She touched one of the intricate ap-
pliquéd squares. The detail was incredible and she
wondered if Louisa had made it. Then she saw the LM
stitched along the edge.

Again she glanced around the suite. It was all so
perfect. And she didn't belong here.

There was still time to leave. She had time to tell
Louisa that she'd changed her mind.

She swung around as Marta walked in, pulling her
wheeled suitcase. "Are you sure this is my room?" Jade
asked.

She smiled. "*Sí, señorita. Señora* Louisa told me to put your clothes in this one so you are close to her. She's across the hall."

That could also mean Jade would be close to Clayton Merrick. "Doesn't her husband also stay there? I mean, I don't want to disturb them."

Marta shook her head. "Oh, no. Not since the *Señora* Louisa had her stroke."

Jade had a lot of questions about the senator, but decided they could wait. "I see."

Marta finished hanging her clothes in the closet. Since Jade had worn uniforms for work, her personal wardrobe was minimal to say the least, so the task was done quickly.

"How long does Louisa usually nap?"

Marta closed the dresser drawer. "About one hour." She smiled. "Today she might be awake sooner." Marta took Jade's hand. "Thank you, *señorita,* for coming here. *Mi prima* needs you to help make her better."

This was the hard part for Jade. During their phone conversations, she'd gotten to like Louisa, but it suddenly hit Jade now how much her news could affect everyone. More than likely she'd be tossed out once they discovered who she really was. That was if the senator even believed her story. But still she'd come this far and needed to meet her father.

To meet Senator Clay Merrick.

The housekeeper opened the doors to the small terrace, then left the room.

"Thank you, Marta," Jade called to her.

"De nada." The housekeeper closed the door behind her.

Jade sighed and sat down on the chair at the desk. It had only been in the past six months that she discovered her life had been a lie. Going through important documents, after her mother's death, Jade had been shocked to find adoption papers.

Renee Hamilton wasn't her biological mother.

Another shock, she found the name of Kathryn Lowery listed as her birth mother, but the father, unknown. She'd also found a copy of Kathryn Lowery's journal.

Jade reached in her purse and took out the old manila envelope that had been in her mother's safe-deposit box. Inside were the only clues to her real identity. She stared down at the thirty-year-old photo. It was a group picture, but two people stood out. An attractive woman who looked to be in her early twenties. She stood out because the resemblance to Jade was uncanny. Kathryn had the same eyes as her daughter.

The man was a little older, maybe in his late twenties. He had sandy-brown hair and dark eyes with a cleft in his chin. Jade touched the matching dimple in her own chin.

She didn't need to know the man's name because in the backdrop of the picture was a large banner that read, Clay Merrick for U.S. Senate.

Almost immediately after she found the papers, Jade had gone in search of Kathryn Lowery and discovered she once lived in Austin, but had died twenty years ago with complications from pneumonia.

It had been easier to research Clay Merrick since he was a public figure. She'd discovered that he'd been married thirty years ago when he was involved with Kathryn Lowery. Had that been the reason he'd pushed her aside?

Kathryn's journal hadn't said much, only how much

she'd loved Clay. She'd worried about Merrick's career, and she'd agonized over giving her baby away.

Jade's chest tightened feeling the rejection all over again. Had Kathryn even had the chance to tell Clay about the pregnancy? Had he been the one to insist she give the baby away?

This had been what brought Jade to the River's End Ranch—and the nursing job—and to the very real possibility that Clay Merrick was her father. She wasn't even sure she could confront the man. If she did, would he listen to her, or would he deny it all?

Jade folded the picture and put it away. All she knew was she couldn't give up until she discovered the truth.

Later that afternoon, Sloan finally got hold of the senator.

"You should have been here to hire Mom's nurse," Sloan said as Jade Hamilton was getting settled in upstairs.

"It was your mother who wanted to do this, son. Why, is there a problem with who she hired?"

Only that Jade Hamilton was far too distracting for him. "No, so far as I can see. But you should still be here."

"I'll be home as soon as I possibly can," Clay answered. "Just after the vote comes to the floor."

Sloan knew the senator's sense of duty. He also knew Clay loved Louisa, but lately he hadn't been around much. Of course Louisa hadn't been very receptive to her husband since her stroke. She had pushed Clay out of her bed, her room and practically out of her life.

"I thought they had enough votes without you being there."

"How would it look if I'm not here working for my state?"

"What about being here for Mom?"

There was a long sigh. "I talk to Louisa every day. She doesn't have a problem waiting another week until we recess." There was a pause. "Of course, if there were someone to replace me here at the capitol, I could retire and be home full-time."

Clay had hinted about Sloan taking his senate seat since college. "Well, you're going to have to look elsewhere, because I'm happy right here." His father already knew that. Sloan had been involved in breeding free range cattle for the past five years, and that suited him totally.

"Think about how much more you could do if you came to Washington. You could promote your projects. Maybe find some funding for research on drought tolerant grasses."

Wouldn't the cattle industry love that, especially when he was promoting hormone free beef, Sloan thought. It was times like this, he felt he was letting his father down. "Sorry, Dad. Have you thought about Alisa taking your place?"

"Son, your sister's only been out of college a few years." There was a pause. "Of course, she's been pretty vocal on some issues. And there is the fact she is a natural born charmer."

And even though Clay had never made him feel different, Sloan was aware he wasn't a true Merrick, not by blood.

Clay had accepted and loved the eight-year-old boy when he married Louisa, then adopted him a year later. And Sloan adored his younger half sister. "Alisa would be the best choice to carry on the family legacy."

"Or...you can find the perfect woman and make me a grandfather. And I can start preparing my grand-child."

Sloan heard the humor in Clay's voice, but some-thing told him the older man was serious. Suddenly Jade Hamilton came to mind. "I'd really have to rush things along."

"I'm sure your mother would be willing to help you find someone."

Had that been the reason Louisa was so eager to have Jade here? Well, darn. Was his mother playing matchmaker?

He shook off the thought. "Are you at least coming home to meet Mother's new nurse?"

"I'm sure you hired a competent person." Com-motion came over the line and his father said, "Look, Sloan, I've got to go. They need me back in the cham-ber."

As soon as Sloan hung up, the phone from the barn rang. "Yeah, Bud. What do you need?"

"An extra pair of hands. Polly is having trouble with her foal. The vet is on his way, but it looks to be an hour or so before he gets here."

"I'll be right down." Sloan came around the desk and was headed out when he saw Jade Hamilton coming down the staircase.

"Mr. Merrick, may I talk with you? It's about your mother's schedule."

"It'll have to be later." He hurried down the hall, past the dining room and through the kitchen. He grabbed his hat off the peg at the back door and turned around.

"This is important."

"Do you think I don't know that? But this ranch is

my responsibility, too. Right now there are other pressing matters I need to look into." He paused. Maybe he
should show her what life was like out here. "Unless
you want to help."

She looked up at him with those big green eyes. "At
what?"

He had trouble turning away, but knew he'd better.
"Come on." He grabbed her hand and pulled her along.
"I have a foal to deliver."

"You're kidding. You want my help."

"You are a nurse, aren't you?" He walked at a fast
pace but she managed to keep up as he hurried down
the road to the barn. "Polly is having some trouble. No
vet around to help, so you're all I got."

Before Jade could say any more, he nudged her
inside the large structure. The place smelled of horses
and fresh straw, but everything was neat and orderly,
the way he liked things. They continued down a wide
center aisle, past several stalls until they reached the
large birthing pen in the corner.

His mare was already down in fresh straw, and her
breathing was labored. "Hey, Bud. Has there been any
change?"

The foreman shook his head. "She hasn't made any
progress."

Jade looked at the large rust-colored animal. Okay,
she was out of her element with this, but she found she
couldn't just stand there, either. She stepped through
the gate and went to the horse's head, knelt down and
began to stroke her neck. "Hey, there, girl. It's not going
too well, is it?" She glanced at Sloan. "Well, it'll be
over soon."

He felt a strange connection with her. As if they
could handle this together.

He quickly turned toward his foreman. "Bud, this is Mother's nurse, Jade Hamilton. Jade, Bud."

"Ma'am," he said in greeting.

"Hello, Bud."

The horse raised its head and whinnied as if to say, "What about me?"

Rolling up his sleeves, Sloan washed up and poured disinfectant on his hands and arms. He looked at Jade, finding she was helping. "Keep doing what you're doing. I need her to stay calm."

Jade nodded.

He knelt down by the horse's tail and began talking softly to the horse. After another contraction eased, he reached inside the animal and soon said, "Got it. I have a front leg." He worked hard over the next few minutes to help progress things. Sweat beaded on his face. "Yeah, there's the other."

Jade kept talking to Polly.

"Get behind me, Bud, and help."

The foreman wasn't as big as Sloan, but he wrapped his muscular arms around Sloan's middle, dug his boots into the floor and together they pulled. Their work began to pay off when the hooves appeared. "Come on, Polly, help us here," Sloan groaned. There was another contraction and more of the legs showed, then a muzzle.

"Well, looky here," Bud said.

"Come on, sweetheart." Jade got into the act. "Let's show 'em what you can do."

With another hard tug from Sloan, the foal was out. He released the legs and let both mama and baby rest. "It's a filly."

A cheer went up in the gallery as some of the ranch hands began to gather around. "Great job, boss."

"Great job, Polly," Jade added as she continued to stroke the exhausted animal.

Sloan's gaze caught hers. "I guess this wasn't in your job description, huh?"

She smiled. "I guess not, but I'd call it an added bonus. I've seen my share of babies being born, but nothing like this. Thank you."

He seemed surprised by her words. "You're welcome."

Jade climbed to her feet and brushed off her slacks, not caring she'd probably ruined her best pair.

Sloan was washing off when he handed Jade a towel. "You want to do the honors?" He nodded to the filly.

They turned toward the foal as she was starting to stand. Jade began to wipe the animal down. Then Sloan pulled her back as the mare decided to stand up.

"Be careful," he warned. "Polly is gentle but she's also a new mama." They moved toward the other side of the pen, and finished the job on the foal, then nudged her toward her mother's tit to feed.

"Good job, Miss Jade," Bud said, coming up to her. "I think Polly liked having another female around."

"Thank you," she acknowledged to the older man who looked as if he'd spent years in the sun.

"Hey, what about me?" Sloan said. "I had something to do with the birthing."

"And you had my help, kid. Remember I had all the muscle behind you." He smiled brightly, showing off the lines around his eyes.

"And I was holding on to a slippery foal."

Jade could easily see the closeness of the two men. It was obvious how much they cared about each other. She hadn't experienced many friendships outside her mother, and Jim Hamilton had been gone from her life shortly after Jade's arrival.

Renee had health issues by the time Jade reached high school. She hadn't had the time for friends with her mother's advancing MS.

Even when Jade began her career, she'd still spent more time with her mother than friends, except Carrie Bradley. Even Carrie had caused some jealousy with her mother.

She suddenly heard her name. "What?"

Sloan was watching her. "I said, you came through. Thank you." He glanced over her messy attire. "If Marta can't work her miracle, then I owe you a blouse and pants."

"It's okay."

"It would be wise to wear jeans during your time here," he told her.

"Why, will there be more deliveries?"

Sloan didn't want to like this woman. As far as he was concerned, she was an intruder. "Maybe if you're good at your job you'll be able to get my mother back on a horse."

Horseback riding! "I didn't know that was in my job description, either."

Sloan frowned. "You don't ride?"

She straightened. "Maybe once or twice as a kid. I was raised in the city."

"You were raised in Texas."

Bud chimed in. "A few lessons and I bet you'll be a natural."

"I don't have time for lessons. My time here is to be spent with Mrs. Merrick."

The foreman pushed his hat back off his forehead, showing off his salt and pepper hair. "I'd say once you get to know Miss Louisa you'll realize how hard she is to keep up with. She was a very active woman. Her stroke slowed her down some, but with your help, we're hopin' she'll be back to normal real soon."

"I'll be working on that. I'll know more after I talk with her doctor." Jade tried not to think about how her deception could affect Louisa. She wanted to blame everything on Clay Merrick, but she knew that she could have gone to Washington to talk to the man, but she'd chickened out.

Instead when she found this job and put in an application, she'd been totally surprised Louisa called her back. After a short talk, she asked her to come to the ranch for an interview.

"My mother's a very determined woman," Sloan said. "But she's not ready to be cut loose on her own yet. So you can't let her ride roughshod over you, either."

"I'm not a pushover, Mr. Merrick. I know how to handle my patients."

"Mr. Merrick," Bud repeated and began to laugh. "There hasn't been anyone here called Mr. Merrick since Sam, your grandfather." Bud pushed Sloan's hat playfully. "It's just Senator and Sloan."

Sloan shook his head. "We're pretty informal around here."

"So it's first names and wear jeans," Jade said.

"And boots," Bud added. "You don't want to walk around a barn and horses without boots on."

This time she laughed, no matter how much she didn't want to.

"We've lived here twenty-six years last May," Louisa said as they sat at the supper table that evening. The meal was in the garden room off the kitchen, another space with lots of windows. A large glass-top table and comfortable chairs was the central feature. Clay pots were filled with live plants that lined the open windows, inviting in the pleasant fall weather.

"Back then, Samuel and Alice Merrick were still alive and this was the area's largest cattle ranch. And this house resembled a mausoleum. It was very formal and cold." Louisa smiled at her son. "Then Clay brought us here to live."

Jade forced a smile, not wanting to think about her father adopting another man's child, when he'd abandoned his own daughter. But had he even known about Kathryn's pregnancy?

She shook away any negative thoughts. She was here now, in this house, and so close to finding out who she was. And she had no idea what would happen next.

Her first day had been an interesting one. Once Louisa had woken from her nap, they'd gone into the exercise room that had every piece of equipment imaginable. Jade had to work hard to get Louisa focused on the routine she was supposed to do daily. The woman was in very good shape for her age of fifty-eight, even after a stroke, but exercise would help tremendously for her recovery.

And it helped Jade's conscience that Louisa wouldn't be helpless when she left. She did not doubt that when her true identity was discovered, she wouldn't be welcomed any longer.

She closed her eyes. It wasn't supposed to be this way. It was Clay Merrick who should have answered the door—and been the one to interview her. She'd had a plan to confront him. To question him about her mother and why he left. Now, she wasn't sure what to do next.

Louisa spoke up. "Since you've helped bring a foal into the world, you'll probably be bored tomorrow." She turned to her son. "Unless you have something else in mind for Jade."

Jade felt heat rush to her face. "Louisa, I'm here for you," she insisted. "It's whatever you want me to help you with."

"I'm flexible with my schedule. And I'm happy you were there for Polly," Louisa said. "That chestnut is a favorite of mine." With a sigh, she went on. "It seems like yesterday that she was a foal. Where does the time go?"

"Mother, Polly's only three years old," Sloan reminded her. "And if you hadn't been asleep, I would have had you there, too. Next time, I'll make sure of it."

Louisa smiled. Jade doubted much happened around here without this woman knowing about it.

Had she known about her husband's past? Had he ever told her about Kathryn Lowery? Did he still have affairs with younger women?

"Jade…"

She jumped, realizing someone had called her name.

"Excuse me. Did you say something?"

"Are you feeling all right?" Louisa asked and nodded toward the plate of enchiladas. "Is the food okay?"

"Oh, yes, it's delicious." She glanced at Marta as she came into the dining room. "I guess I'm a little tired."

Louisa frowned. "That's right, you came all the way from Dallas, and here we put you right to work. We could have waited a day or two."

Jade smiled. "No, really, I'm fine. Please, don't

worry about me. I came here for a job, so I planned on starting right away."

Sloan watched Jade Hamilton. Even exhausted, the woman was beautiful. She looked more like a model than a nurse. It still puzzled him to why she was here. A rural ranch outside of Kerry Springs wasn't exactly an exciting place to live.

"I hope you don't regret being so far away from everyone and everything familiar," he said. "A small town has a lot of disadvantages."

"And it has a lot of advantages, too," she told him. "Such as no five o'clock traffic, which means no crazy drivers."

"We also have no nightlife."

"Drinking in bars can be overrated," she argued.

"What about fine dining?"

Jade smiled. "I heard that Rory's Bar and Grill has great barbecue."

Sloan nodded. "The best."

Louisa jumped in. "Son, you'll have to take Jade in to give her a sample."

Great, he'd walked into that one. "Ms. Hamilton needs to focus on you."

Those beautiful eyes widened. He suddenly wondered what else he could get her to react to. Whoa, he needed to take a step back. This was an employee, his mother's nurse.

He stood. "I should check on the filly."

"Why don't you take Jade along?" his mother suggested. "I mean, she did help deliver her."

Jade shook her head. "No. I need to stay with you."

Louisa shrugged. "I'm going to watch television with Marta. If I need to go upstairs, there's the elevator." She waved her arm. "Now, go. You're dying to see that foal again."

Jade relented.

Sloan shot his mother a disapproving look, but it didn't seem to faze her. He waited for Jade to head out the door first, turned back and spoke in Spanish. *"Basta, Madre."*

She smiled up at him. "Enough what, dear?"

He ignored her innocent look as he met up with Jade. The evening was cool and he handed her a jacket from the hook near the back door.

"Here, you better put this on," he said as he held it out for her. When she slipped her arms in, he caught a whiff of her perfume, a fresh citrus scent.

"The first thing to know about my mother is that she likes getting her way."

She glanced at him as they headed toward the barn. "What woman doesn't?"

"But Louisa is relentless when she sets her mind to something. Just don't let her get away with anything."

"You forget it was your mother who wanted me here. She's the one who wants to recover."

He opened the door to the barn and paused as he found himself leaning closer to her. In less than twenty-four hours, she'd managed to draw him in, made him want and need. Damn, if she wasn't the most tempting woman. He quickly roped in his desire and managed to speak. "Don't say I didn't warn you."

He motioned for her to walk in ahead of him. Mistake. He tried not to stare at her shapely backside, but lost the fight and enjoyed the view as they made their way down the aisle toward the last pen. It was quiet and that was how he liked things. Polly spotted him and blew out a long breath in greeting. "How are you doing, girl?"

The chestnut made her way to the gate and let Sloan rub her muzzle. "You had quite a day, Mama." He glanced down at the filly. "Well, hello to you, too, little one."

He lowered his hand, but it was Jade who got the attention. The filly with the white star on her forehead came toward her. "I guess you females stick together."

Jade knelt down and coaxed the filly with her hand. "It's my voice. It's softer. Oh, she's so cute."

That wasn't the only soft thing about Jade. He glanced away from the soft skin of her cheeks, only to catch the generous curve of her backside. He released a frustrated breath. He needed to get out more and get away from a certain pretty nurse, or he might be in some big trouble.

CHAPTER THREE

THE next morning, Sloan was out of the house and on his way to the barn before dawn. Over the next two hours he worked alongside the other hands to feed livestock and set up the work schedule for the day before he finally came in for breakfast.

Five years ago after college, he'd moved out of the main house. He'd built his own place just up the road about a quarter of a mile. The one thing he did was come by occasionally and share breakfast with his mother. After her stroke and his father's return to Washington, he'd stayed over, temporarily, when his sister was out of town.

Now there was Nurse Jade on the premises so he could go back to his place. In truth, Jade Hamilton was a distraction. He couldn't even walk past her bedroom door this morning without pausing, hoping to see her again. Still, he told himself he needed to wait a little longer to see how things worked out. He'd stay here a few more nights.

A pretty woman arriving in Kerry Springs sent up several warning signals for him. Although the feelings had gone cold, the bad memories were still raw. The difference this time from the last, he planned to keep his distance.

He wasn't the only one who'd been intrigued by the nurse. He'd seen how the ranch hands had watched her yesterday in the barn. It was not what he needed right now with the fall roundup coming soon. All ranch hands needed to focus on their jobs.

That included him. This was the future of River's End. His chance to prove to Clay that he could make the ranch thrive. His way.

He headed up the porch steps to the back door. After scraping his boots, he walked in and hung his hat on the hook. He found Marta at the stove and greeted her, but before he could ask about his mother, he heard voices coming from the garden room. As he entered, he saw something he hadn't seen in a while.

A happy Louisa Merrick. Then his attention went to her companion.

Jade looked fresh and pretty this morning. Her hair was pulled back from her face, exposing her creamy skin, pert nose and delicate jaw. Then she smiled and it caused his heart rate to accelerate.

"This is crazy," he mumbled and walked in.

His mother saw him first. "Sloan, I was wondering where you were."

"I was working. Remember, there's a ranch to run."

His mother frowned. "Someone is grumpy this morning. I told you, son, you need more leisure time. You can't let this place consume you."

He glanced at Jade. At least he could be cordial. "Mornin', Jade."

"Good morning, Sloan," she answered in a soft voice.

He dished up eggs and hash browns onto his plate. "Maybe I'll feel better once I have some breakfast."

"You always were grouchy when you were hungry."

He swallowed a big bite. "Well, that should be fixed soon." He wanted to change the subject. "What are your plans today?"

Louisa looked proud of herself. "We've already been working. Jade talked with my therapist when she came by earlier, so she can help me with my daily exercises." Louisa glanced at Jade. "And since I've been such a good patient, after breakfast we're going into town. I have a hair appointment in an hour."

He nearly choked on his food. Hadn't the family been trying for weeks to get her into town? "A hair appointment?"

"Don't you think it's about time I do something with this mess?" She pointed to her dark hair streaked with gray pulled back into a ponytail.

He shot a look at Jade, wondering how she'd talked Louisa into this. "You always look beautiful, Mom, but I agree this will make you feel better."

"Good. So don't expect us home for lunch because we have more plans. And we may just stop by the Blind Stitch, too."

He shook his head. "Whoa, I don't think you should overdo it. It's been a while since you've spent the day out."

Louisa studied her son. "I know you're concerned, but I'll let Jade know if it's too much for me. Now I need to go upstairs and get ready."

Jade immediately got up as did Sloan.

"No, both of you finish your breakfast. I can manage." Louisa reached for her walker. "Besides, I'm sure you have questions for Jade. Don't bully her."

They watched her leave, then Sloan motioned for Jade to sit down.

Jade braced herself.

"Don't you think you're moving too fast?"

"I wouldn't do anything without checking with your mother's doctor," she said confidently. "Dr. Carstairs returned my call about thirty minutes ago. He agrees it would be good for Louisa to get out of the house. In fact he's been suggesting that to her for the past month."

Sloan continued to stare at her. "Seems you've worked a miracle."

She cocked her head. "Are you upset because you're worried about your mother, or that I'm the one who got her to go into town?"

He seemed to relax a little. "Maybe both. She hasn't exactly been in an agreeable mood lately."

She nodded. "Yes, your mother is stubborn. I've come to realize sometimes it's easier for a person to confide in a stranger, than ask help from family."

"My mother can be a handful when she wants to be."

"Perhaps she enjoys the attention?"

"That's Mom." He sighed. "A lot of people envy her, but she hasn't had a perfect life. Being married to a political icon hasn't been easy. Although, she's never been a fan of D.C. lifestyle and all the politics. She was born and bred in Texas. It's her home. She's always been more comfortable on the ranch with her family around her." He studied Jade. "All in all, she's a private person. Alisa and I are, too."

Jade couldn't help but hear a little animosity in his voice, she was also distracted about the possibility of having a half sister. So far she'd only seen a few pictures of Alisa Merrick up in Louisa's bedroom. She wanted answers to so many things, but Sloan wasn't the one to ask.

All she needed to do now was her job. Already, she'd gotten more involved with this family than she should, or had any right to. But she found a glimpse had made her want more.

That didn't seem to keep her from asking, "Doesn't the senator usually come home on the weekends?"

He nodded, but there was the suspicious look. "He's staying in D.C. now because of an important vote coming up. He'll be home in another week. I handle ranch business and any family business. Why? Is there a reason he should come sooner?"

Jade shook her head. "No. Only that it might lift your mother's spirits."

"Being apart from her husband is something my mother has had to deal with during their entire marriage." He took a drink of coffee. "Merricks have been in public service for years. We should have all moved to D.C. years ago.

"Why didn't you?"

He glared, then finally answered, "Because our mother didn't want to take me and my sister from a normal life with our friends and school."

She studied him for a moment. If anyone belonged here on the ranch, it was Sloan. "I can't see you living in Washington, either. You seem to love this place too much."

He smiled and she felt a warm rush. It quickly died. "Not everyone feels that way."

Jade put down her fork. She wasn't hungry any longer. She was itching to dig for more information. To get insight into her father. Instead she decided to only let Sloan talk if he wanted. "Isn't your father happy that you're running the ranch?"

He shook his head. "What made you think it's my father?"

She opened her mouth to deny it, but couldn't come out with the words.

"You're somewhat right. Dad hasn't taken much interest in ranching in a long time. Since I inherited my section of land on the ranch, I'm raising my own free-range cattle. I'm also experimenting with a drought-tolerant grass, which can stand up to our brutal Texas summers."

She raised an eyebrow. So he wasn't just a good-looking cowboy. "I'm impressed."

He shrugged, then seemed to realize that he'd opened up to her. "Just testing right now."

"Would I get fired if I said I don't eat beef?"

His eyes narrowed. "It's a free world."

"I thought that would be a capital offense around here." She tried to joke, but he didn't seem to think it was humorous.

She stood and carried her plate into the kitchen, came back with the coffeepot and filled his mug and hers. "Sloan, you can be assured of one thing, I will always put your mother's needs first."

Jade sat back down. "Her stroke has been a big hit to her pride. She's lucky. She should recover fully and lead a normal life."

He shook his head. "Oh, Jade, why would she start now? Louisa Cruz Sloan Merrick never has before."

Two hours later while Louisa was having her hair done at Sissy's Scissor Salon in town, Jade took off to the drugstore to buy some personal items. Then to the general store where she purchased two pairs of jeans, some cotton blouses and T-shirts.

Since she'd been hired on the spot yesterday, she hadn't had time to prepare for anything. Not for moving into the Merrick home, or having Louisa take her in as if they were long lost friends. At this point, she wasn't sure how things would turn out. She hadn't thought that far ahead. Honestly, she was a little afraid to know the outcome.

Thirty minutes later, she'd taken the shopping bag back to the black town car that Sloan insisted they take for their outing. The driver was Marta's husband, Miguel, who was sitting on a bench in the shade.

With a smile, the middle-aged man took her purchases and placed them in the trunk. It amazed her how the Merrick family lived. It was so different from how she grew up in the small rental house in Dallas.

She couldn't help but wonder if things would have been altered if Clay knew about her? Whoa, was she even his daughter? Yet, even though she didn't have any proof, everything led her to believe she was a Merrick.

So would the state's favorite son be forgiven for his past indiscretions? As far as she could tell, no one had a bad word to say about Clay or the family. Over the years, he'd helped pass legislation that had been beneficial for the state, especially the ranchers.

Was the man still a womanizer? Her own research hadn't brought up a single story of him being unfaithful, or doing anything unethical. Of course, she knew otherwise.

Jade walked back to the salon and found Louisa sporting a new short haircut, her face glowing with a subtle amount of makeup.

"You look amazing," Jade said.

The thirty-something hairdresser and owner, Sissy

Henderson added, "I've been trying to talk Miss Louisa into this cut forever. Doesn't she look years younger?"

Louisa made a groaning sound. "The cane kind of gives away my age."

"That'll be gone soon," Jade told her.

She'd talked Louisa into leaving the walker at home and using the cane today. She'd handled it right off. "With the way you're attacking your exercises, I'll give it a few weeks."

That brought a smile. "I'm going to hold you to that."

They started for the door. "I bet the senator is going to flip over your new look. If so, you owe me a big tip." Sissy winked and gave a wave as they walked out.

Sadness showed on Louisa's face as they headed for the sidewalk. "It would be a first in a long time," she murmured.

Jade caught the words and didn't react to them. "Where to next? The Blind Stitch."

Louisa hesitated. "Maybe that isn't a good idea today."

Jade was concerned about her change of heart. "Are you feeling okay?"

"A little tired."

"They're your friends, Louisa. They love you and miss you. And I think you miss them, too."

"I do." They made their way down the street and ended up at the quilt shop's storefront. "It's just that things have changed. I've changed."

"Not inside. You're still the same in your heart. That's what they love about you."

Suddenly the shop door opened and Jenny appeared. "Louisa Merrick, don't you dare walk by without stopping in."

Louisa's face lit up. "Well, Jenny Rafferty, I guess you weren't going to let me even if I tried."

"You got that right." The young woman hugged Louisa. "You look wonderful. Oh, my, I love the new do." She nodded toward her hair. "So youthful."

Louisa laughed. "I must have looked like an old hag."

"Oh, you couldn't if you tried." She turned to Jade. "Hi, Jade. Thank you for bringing her by."

"You're welcome."

Louisa waved a hand. "Wait a minute. Have I been set up?"

Jenny opened the door wider. "As if we could get anything past you. Come on in, the girls are anxious to see you."

Louisa relented and made her way inside. Jenny led them through the store and into the connecting room where at a round table in the corner there were four women. "Ladies, look who's here."

With a squeal, the group of women got out of their chairs and hurried toward them. After several hugs and a few tears, Louisa composed herself, then introduced the group. "Jade, this is Beth, Liz, Lisa and Caitlin. The girls from the Quilters' Corner. Jade is my nurse."

They exchanged greetings with her, then someone asked, "Do you quilt, Jade?"

She shook her head. "I mostly watched my mother, and that was years ago."

Another woman walked over. "Then we'll have to get you involved with us." She smiled at Jade. "Hi, I'm Millie, and I work here. I could get you started on something simple. Louisa can bring you in."

Jade shook her head. "I think I'm staying pretty busy right now."

"Yeah, Louisa is a handful, all right."

Everyone laughed, including Louisa who said, "I can see how much you girls missed me."

Beth stepped up. "You can't believe how much. Dang, woman, I'm so glad you're back."

"I'm not back exactly. I still have a bum hand. I can't make a stitch worth a darn."

Jade could see how hard that was for her to admit.

"Come anyway, and sort fabrics, stamp blocks, use the cutter," Millie said. "We just want your company."

Jade could see that Louisa was touched. "You do need someone to keep you all working. How are the hospital baby quilts coming?"

"We're a little behind. And there's two babies due at the end of November."

Louisa turned to Jade. "We make quilts for all the newborns born in the area."

"Oh, my, how do you keep up?"

"We aren't a big community," the woman named Liz admitted. "But I have a feeling that Jenny and Evan aren't going to wait too long before they add to our town's population."

With that said Jenny's face reddened. "We've only been married a few months."

Beth spoke up. "I see you eyeing those babies that come in here. You want one, and when a woman wants a baby, a man doesn't stand a chance."

Jenny blushed so badly that Jade felt sorry for her. "Just put in your order for the color so we can get started early."

The bell over the door sounded and Jenny let out a breath. "Thank you, I need to go back to work. Nice to see you again, Jade. Hope you'll come back so we can visit longer."

"I'd like that," she said, and discovered she wanted to get to know her.

Jenny made her escape as Louisa announced, "We were going to lunch. Who wants to go? My treat."

"We all do," Beth joked. "And I vote for Rory's Bar and Grill. Sean Rafferty is working today. That's Jenny's good-looking father-in-law." She raised an eyebrow. "As my granddaughter would say, he's some 'eye candy.'"

The women laughed and Jade wondered if she could keep up with these ladies. She'd soon find out.

With a wave, Jenny called out, "Behave. And enjoy yourselves."

They headed down the street only about a block. Jade kept a close watch on Louisa, but she seemed to be doing fine. They crossed with the streetlight and filed into the restaurant.

The inside was dim and there were several patrons seated along the long oak bar. But the women took interest in the one male behind the bar, a tall man with thick white hair, an easy smile and a twinkle in his light eyes. He waved and the women giggled.

Beth directed them to a large circular booth toward the back. After they filed in, Jade situated Louisa on the end, then got a chair and sat down at the head of the table.

"Did you see him?" Liz said.

"Of course we did," Louisa said. "Sean's a big man."

Everyone turned as the man in question walked over toward them. For his age of about sixty, Sean was handsome and kept himself in shape.

"Saints preserve us, I've died and gone to heaven,"

Sean said. "What did I do to be blessed with you lovely lassies today?"

And charming, Jade thought.

"It's just your lucky day, Sean Rafferty," Louisa said.

"My, oh, my. The lovely Louisa." Concern showed on his face. "It surely is good to see you out and about, and looking so well."

Louisa nodded. "Living a good, clean life."

He flashed a quick wink. "I'll have to talk to the senator about that."

That brought a hoot from the girls.

Jade found she was enjoying this. No wonder the women liked this man.

"And who is this lovely?" The big Irishman took her hand. "I'm Sean Rafferty, at your service."

"Jade Hamilton."

"She's just arrived in town," Louisa said. "She's staying with me out at the ranch."

"A pretty name for a pretty woman. I believe I have someone who would be interested in meeting you." He glanced toward the bar and motioned to a guy. As the younger man strolled toward the group. Jade saw the resemblance right away. The difference was in the younger cowboy's coloring. He had dark hair and killer bedroom eyes. Oh, and a wicked grin.

"Jade, this is my son, Matthew. Matt, Jade Hamilton, she's just arrived in town. And you know all the other ladies."

Matt was polite, and greeted the older women first, then turned his attention to her. "Jade. It's definitely a pleasure to meet you. I hope you enjoy Kerry Springs enough to stay around for a while."

"From what I've seen, I do like it here."

"That's wonderful news. And if you need anyone to show you around, I'm definitely available."

"Thank you, Matt." She was nervous with everyone watching her. "I'm going to be pretty busy for the next few weeks."

"Yes, she'll be working," a familiar voice answered. Everyone turned to see Sloan.

Jade nearly groaned. What was he doing here?

"Hey, Merrick," Matt said. "How's it going?"

There wasn't any handshakes exchanged between them. It was more of a standoff. "Not bad," Sloan said as he glanced at Jade. "And it's getting better by the second. You?"

"Working hard, and just trying to stay out of trouble."

"Glad to hear it."

Louisa spoke up. "Sloan, please tell me you haven't been following me."

He shook his head. "I came into town to pick up my order at the feed store. I saw Miguel and thought I'd stop and say hello." He tipped his hat. "Ladies, I'm sorry to interrupt."

They all smiled. This was the last thing she'd expected. For a small town there sure was a lot of testosterone floating around.

Then Sloan's gaze went to Jade, causing her breath to catch. What was that about?

He finally turned to Louisa. "Mother, just don't overdo it."

"Not a chance of that with everyone hovering."

Again he nodded. "I'll leave you all to your lunch." He started to leave, then paused and said, "Hey, Rafferty, I need to talk to you about the roundup."

Matt said goodbye, but his gaze lingered on Jade. "Maybe we'll run into each other again."

Jade wasn't sure what to say, so she nodded.

Sean was the only man left now. "I take it you ladies all want the barbecue lunch special?" With their nod, he said, "And a pitcher of iced tea."

"That's perfect, Sean," Louisa said. "Thank you."

When he walked off, Beth spoke up. "I'll pick up the check today, Louisa. I haven't had this much entertainment in years." She glanced at Jade. "Don't look now, darlin' but looks like you caught a couple of live ones."

Louisa had a smile on her face, too.

"I'm not here to catch a guy," Jade stressed. "I'm here to help Louisa."

"It doesn't look like you have a choice." Liz sighed. "Oh, I remember those days when my Randy used to chase after me, trying to get my attention."

With their nods, they watched as Sean went behind the bar.

"Isn't he something," Beth said.

"Don't let Millie hear you saying that," Liz said. "She's had a thing for Sean for years."

"A lot of good it does her," Beth told her. "The man hasn't dated much. Do you think he has someone in San Antonio?"

"Who cares?" Lisa said. "I think we have more love budding closer to home." She smiled at Jade. "Two men. And to think I thought life was getting boring around here, and then you come to town."

CHAPTER FOUR

Two hours later, Jade brought Louisa home from town and talked her into taking a nap. Even though she insisted that she wasn't tired from her outing, the older woman fell right to sleep once she lay back against the pillow.

Jade stayed a few minutes to make sure she was truly asleep, then left. She would have gone to her own room to relax, but found she was too keyed up to stay inside. She had had a great time with Louisa and her friends today, until Sloan showed up. Did he follow them? Did he not trust her?

Going down to the kitchen, she asked Marta if she would listen for Louisa.

When the housekeeper agreed, Jade walked out the back door to the porch to enjoy the late afternoon fall day. The sights and sounds of the operation were evident. She watched the ranch hands on horseback shout commands as they moved cattle into large holding pens.

This was her father's life. He'd been born and raised on this ranch. Yet she'd been denied this life. Kathryn chose not to tell Clay about her. As a child Jade had daydreamed about a father. She never got the chance to know any more about Jim Hamilton than that he never wanted anything to do with her and left the marriage.

Would Clay have accepted her as his daughter if he'd known about her? Did he know about her and walk away anyway? She couldn't help but wonder what it would have been like to come here to live.

She sighed. She couldn't think about that. She hadn't had a perfect life growing up but there was never a doubt that Mother loved her. Still the past few months had been difficult, trying to grasp the fact that her identity had all been a lie. She wasn't a Hamilton, and there was a good possibility she was a Merrick. Was it crazy to want to know where she'd come from? To discover who she was.

Curious about ranch life, she was itching to go out and experience it all. But she didn't want to get in anyone's way, especially Sloan's. Even though he was only a stepson, he was truly Clay's son. They had a special bond.

What would happen when he learned the real story? The man didn't trust easily. She'd probably be run out of town.

No. She couldn't let anyone find out yet, if ever. Not before she talked to Clay. She was pretty sure how they'd react and right now she'd settle for a little piece of Clay Merrick's life. She stepped off the porch, and headed toward the barn. She decided she wanted to see the filly again.

She walked through the double doors, and found Bud talking with one of the hands. "Well, hello, Jade."

"Hi, Bud. Is it okay to visit the filly?"

His smile turned into a grin. "I don't see why not. Come on, I'll go with you." Together they walked down

to the last stall. Immediately Polly came to the railing to greet them.

Bud spoke up, "Hello, Mama. Look who I brought by to see ya."

The horse made a nickering sound and moved toward Jade. Jade tensed at first, but slowly began to relax recalling their connection during the birthing. "Hi, Polly."

The horse pushed her muzzle against her arm. Jade reached up and began petting the large animal. Polly was eager for some affection. "Hello, girl. How's your baby today?"

The animal bobbed her head and blew out a loud breath.

"Now, that's one happy mama," Bud teased and they both laughed.

"I guess I missed the joke."

They both turned to see Sloan standing in the aisle. He didn't look any happier than he had at Rory's.

"Hey, Sloan," Bud said. "Jade came out to check on Polly."

With one look from Sloan, Jade felt as if she was doing something wrong. "I hope you don't mind."

"Not as long as you don't go wandering around by yourself," he told her. "You aren't used to ranch life."

She felt a sudden anger. That wasn't her fault. "Then I guess I should learn the ins and outs, so I won't get caught in a cattle stampede or something."

"With the roundup scheduled for next week it's going to be busy around here, that's all. You could get hurt."

She straightened. "I'll stay out of the way, Mr. Merrick. I better get back to my responsibilities." She smiled at the foreman. "Thank you, Bud."

"Anytime, darlin', you just call on old Bud."

"Excuse me," she said, then hurried off down the aisle.

Sloan glanced at the disappointment on Bud's face, realizing that he'd spoken harshly. Then he watched Jade until she disappeared through the doors.

"Well, I'm willing to guess your daddy would be ashamed of how you handled that."

Sloan turned back to his foreman. "What? She's my mother's nurse. She shouldn't be out here."

"Why not? Is she chained to the house?" He whipped off his hat. "You didn't have any problem with her out here yesterday when you needed her."

"That was different. We were all here." His words even sounded lame to him. "Besides, she'll be leaving soon."

"I think anyone who has the smarts to go through college and get a degree would be able to find their way around a ranch without getting into trouble." His gaze moved over Sloan. "But maybe not."

"What was that supposed to mean?"

"You're a smart college guy. Seems to me you ought to be able to figure out why one cute, green-eyed filly sets you off."

He stiffened, recalling a different time, a different woman. "I won't be fooled again by a pretty face. It's a waste of time and trouble when all they want to do is change you."

Bud sighed, and pushed his hat back off his forehead. "Now there's your first mistake, son, thinking they're all the same." He glanced down the aisle toward Jade. "I'm thinkin' this one could be a keeper."

It wasn't until the following evening that Sloan conceded Bud had been partly right. His attitude toward

Jade Hamilton had been uncalled for. The only reason he could come up with was the one old Bud hinted about, that the woman was one big distraction. She had only been here a few days, and she'd been in his head constantly. Yet, there was something about her that still nagged at him.

Okay, she was a beautiful woman. He'd seen the interest she'd gotten from other men, including Matt Rafferty. Why had it bothered him? He wanted to think because he was protective of her because of Matt's carousing ways, but he knew the real reason: he was attracted to her, too. That could mean trouble for so many reasons. First and foremost, she was his mother's nurse and he didn't want anything to interfere with his mother's recovery.

Then there was the fact he didn't want to put himself out there again. Once before he'd thought he'd found a woman he could love. Crystal had seemed perfect for him, for the ranch life. Then he learned that he was being used because of the Merrick name. And his bad judgment cost them all a lot.

No. He wasn't about to let that happen again.

He walked through the back door and saw Jade all fresh and pretty. She looked up. Her eyes drew him, causing an awareness that was so strong and so intense he had to work to slow his breathing. He definitely wasn't thinking with his head anymore.

"Hello, son," his mother called, drawing his attention away.

"Oh, hi, Mom." Then he saw piles of fabric squares scattered on the table, and he asked, "How was your afternoon?"

She glanced at him. "Oh, it was lovely. When I saw all the girls yesterday, they convinced me, even if I

can't hand sew right now that I still need to get back into quilting. So Jade's helping me sort through some fabric, and we're pinning it." She shrugged. "Maybe I'll even attempt to use the cutter."

He watched as Louisa awkwardly picked up fabric. Her actions were slow, but she was putting forth the effort, and it was more than he'd seen his mother try in months. His spirits soared. He looked at Jade, hoping to get her attention, but she was busy sorting. Then suddenly she stood, picked up the empty glasses and walked into the kitchen.

Maybe he deserved the cold shoulder. He put on a smile and turned back to his mother. "It's good to see you get excited over a project again. I suspect the ladies were happy to see you."

"They were." Louisa looked sad. "Even though I've been avoiding their calls."

"Mom, you're working through your recovery." He squatted down beside her. "You've been through a lot. All we want is for you to get better."

She touched his cheek. "I've been feeling sorry for myself."

"You had a right." He fought a smile. "Maybe for a little while. But look what you're doing to get back at a hundred percent?"

"Jade has helped me a lot. I'm glad she's here."

He was beginning to realize that, too. "Seems she's getting results where we couldn't help you."

"No, she just doesn't let me get away with anything. Not like you."

He smiled. "Okay, so she's a miracle worker."

Louisa gave him a playful smack, then sobered. "Whatever, she's helped me see a lot of things. If I want to get better, I'm the only one who can do it."

"She's not pushing you too hard, is she?"

"That's just it, son. I need to push myself if I want to get back to how I was." Tears flooded her eyes. "I've been putting you and Alisa through so much with my stubbornness."

"We've survived." In days, Jade Hamilton had accomplished more good than they had in months. "We love you, Mom, and you're worth it."

She looked sad again. "And your father…"

Sloan knew that his mother's stroke had put a strain on their once perfect marriage. It had been hard to watch as she had pulled away from Clay and any offer of help or affection. "Dad will be home soon. Everything will be fine."

She didn't look convinced. "It's only… I'm not the woman he married."

He would never call his mother vain. Yet she had always taken special care of her appearance. She was still a beautiful woman, but he realized that a stroke changes people.

He reached for her hand. "Talk to Dad about how you feel."

She shook her head. "I don't know if I can."

Surely she didn't think that Clay would reject her. "Of course you can." He didn't want to discuss his mother's marriage problems. "You've always told me he's the best listener."

There had been a time during Sloan's adolescence that he'd rejected any of Clay's attempts at being a father. It took a year or so before he trusted the man to be there for him.

"Look, he won't be home for another week. At least think about it. You two have been married a long time."

He smiled. "I happen to know the man is crazy about you."

When he saw his mother smile, he added, "I better let you get back to your project." He stood. "Well, if you don't need anything, I think I'll call it an early night."

His mother looked up and shook her head. "You lead a boring life, son."

"Maybe you're right, but I'm busy trying to get ready for the roundup."

"And you're thirty-two," she retorted. "You should go out more…find that special woman."

He'd been through this before with her. He hadn't had much luck in the relationship department. He wasn't a good judge of character. His choosing Crystal proved that.

"After the roundup."

He kissed her cheek and headed to the kitchen and the back stairway to the second floor. Anxious to get away, he'd barely got out the door when he suddenly collided with someone. Jade.

"Oh," she gasped.

He reached out and caught her around the waist to steady her. Except he wasn't so steady, either, as her body pressed against his.

"You okay?" he managed as she raised those incredible eyes to his.

She released a breath, then quickly broke the hold and stepped back. "I'm fine."

Damn if I am. He still couldn't take his eyes off her. He fought the urge to pull her back, to touch her, to feel her softness against him.

Jade glanced away. "Marta said to tell you she left your supper in the oven."

The hunger he felt deep in his gut had nothing to do with food. "Your eyes are incredible." She was tall and slender, but she had plenty of curves.

She lowered her lashes. "Thank you."

The rest of her was just as incredible, too. "I was thinking of riding out to check my herd tomorrow. Would you like to go?" Where did that come from?

"You mean on a horse?"

He nodded. "It'll soon come back to you."

"Your mother's therapist is coming in the morning for her exercise session. I have to be there."

"Just call down to the barn when you're free."

He glanced down at her sandals. "I'll dig up a pair of my sister's boots." He walked outside and hoped the night air would cool him off before he did something stupid.

Early the next morning, Jade stood next to Louisa in the home gym. The top-of-the-line equipment filled the large room. The therapist had just left and Louisa was finishing up her routine. Jade glanced at her patient and saw the beads of sweat on her face as she worked to raise the small hand weights.

Jade noticed Louisa's range of motion had increased, and her balance was so much better, too. Louisa's hard work on the treadmill and weights over the past few days had paid off.

"Let's take a break," Jade said.

Louisa put down the weights. "What's this 'us' business. Seems I've been doing all the work."

Jade smiled as she checked the woman's heart rate. It was good. She draped the stethoscope around her neck. "And it's showing."

Louisa's breathing wasn't too labored, either. "Not

fast enough," she said to Jade. "I've got other things to do besides hang out in here all day."

Jade raised an eyebrow. "And what exactly are these plans?"

Louisa gave her a sideways glance. "Stop worrying. I've invited the girls here for lunch then we're working on baby quilts."

Jade was glad Louisa was being social again. "Sounds like fun."

"You're welcome to join us."

Jade hesitated. She was supposed to go riding today, but she was having second thoughts about spending more time with Sloan. She'd seen his interest in her, and it would be so easy to reciprocate. Definitely not a good idea. This wasn't why she came here.

"Sure."

Louisa caught her reluctance. "Well, that was heartfelt." She patted the towel on her face and paused. "You're not on the clock all the time, Jade. You're allowed some personal time."

"I know that. I happen to like your friends, but if you'd rather I disappeared…"

Louisa studied her. "Okay, what's going on here?"

"Nothing," she said too quickly. "I mean, you're probably tired of having me glued to your side."

"If I felt that way, I'd tell you," Louisa assured her. "But you don't have to work 24/7, either. You know there are labor laws. And I believe you haven't had any time off since you arrived here The weekend is coming up. You should get out and get to know the area. There's plenty of wineries to the north of us. Jenny's husband, Evan, owns the Rafferty Vineyard. And there's San Antonio."

"I'm not real social. But if it's okay with you, I'd like a few hours off today. I might go riding while you're with your friends."

Louisa blinked in surprise. "Sloan asked you?"

Here it comes. She nodded. "He's checking the herd and thought I'd like to see some of the ranch."

"So he's taking my advice." Louisa's gaze met hers. "I'm glad, because he's worked too hard this past year." She waved her hand. "Go, and make sure you both relax."

"Then since we're finished here, you should hit the showers." Jade handed Louisa her cane and followed her out of the gym and down the hall to her bedroom. She went on ahead into the connecting bath and turned on the water in the large walk-in shower. Once she had Louisa situated, she left the woman to her privacy and went into the bedroom.

The phone rang. When it wasn't answered by Marta on the third ring, Jade picked it up.

"Hello, Merrick residence," she said.

There was a pause. "Who is this?" a man with a deep, rich voice asked.

"Jade Hamilton."

"Oh, so you're the miracle worker I've been hearing about."

"I wouldn't say I was a miracle worker." She felt her heart pounding hard against her ribs. "May I ask who is calling?"

"Clay Merrick."

"Oh, Senator." She nearly choked. "I'm sorry, I didn't know."

"Why? You've never met me. You had no idea who I

was." She heard the smile in his voice. "But I can't wait to meet you."

She swallowed back the dryness in her throat. This was her father. "I've been looking forward to that, too."

CHAPTER FIVE

AN HOUR later, Sloan sat atop his gelding, Amigo, watching closely to see how Jade handled her horse, Cally. The small mare was the gentlest mount on the ranch.

Once outside the corral, they headed through the grove of trees and rode along the dry creek bed. Thanks to the recent autumn rains the plains were a rich green, but the trees on the hillside were changing color into bright, golden hues of red and orange. This was his favorite time of year, when all his hard work paid off.

Suddenly his mother's words came to mind. *You lead a boring life, son.* He'd always worked hard, especially the last eleven months. He'd never been one to order ranch hands to do anything that he wouldn't do. Damn, he was turning into a control freak. Maybe he could use some time off.

He stole a glance at Jade. It had been a long time since a woman had distracted him. Not because he didn't want someone special in his life, but Clay's public life had made it difficult to have much privacy. He was also suspicious of who his true friends...and lovers...were. As the son of a U.S. senator, people had expectations of him.

He expected to feel a pang of sadness over Crystal.

Although she was from San Antonio, he'd thought he knew his former girlfriend better. After being together six months he'd soon discovered that she wanted the Merrick name and money. When they'd broken up she sold her story to the tabloids. He'd learned his lesson the hard way. It just seemed safer to concentrate on his work. The River's End Ranch.

He heard his name called and looked toward Jade again.

"How am I doing?" she asked.

She sat relaxed in the saddle as she moved easily with the horse. He smiled. "Just fine. In fact you look pretty good, which is better for the horse. Believe me, they can sense an inexperienced rider."

"So I'm not too bad for a city gal," she said in an exaggerated twang.

She was a lot better than not bad. "A natural. I think you've ridden more than you said."

"Actually, not so much," she began. "Once my mother saw the size of the horse I'd been riding, she refused to let me continue the classes." Jade glanced at him as their horses walked side by side along the trail. "My parents were older when they got me."

He smiled. "So you were a surprise?"

"Yes and no."

Jade enjoyed watching Sloan. If anyone was born to ranch life, it was this man. He was impressive astride his roan gelding, and handled the large animal with ease and grace. She quickly shook away any wandering thoughts. Gawking at good-looking cowboys wasn't why she came here.

"I was always planned, but I didn't arrive until they were in their late forties." She wasn't willing to tell him everything.

"No wonder they were a little overprotective of you."

"I know. My mother wanted a baby for a long time." She gave him a bright smile. "So giving up riding wasn't so bad, not when my mother bribed me with ballet classes."

"How did you like that?"

She smiled trying to hide her nervousness. "I loved the little outfits better than the dancing. Besides, I soon discovered I had no talent whatsoever, but my friends were in the class so I stuck it out for a few years."

"From where I sit, you look pretty graceful to me."

She was taken aback by his compliment. "You didn't see me at nine when I was all arms and legs. The braces came later."

She caught him studying her and it did funny things to her insides. She took a slow breath, trying to steady her sudden rapid heart rate.

"Well, everything seemed to turn out good," he said. "You're a beautiful woman, Jade Hamilton."

"Thank you." She looked toward the trail. No matter how attracted she was to this man, she couldn't let this go any further.

"So, how far is this herd?"

"I have a turkey and a ham sandwich," Sloan said as he looked into the lunch bag.

"Whatever. I don't care which." Jade sat down on the blanket spread under a big tree beside the creek. Water trickled over the rocky bottom, making a soothing sound. Across on the other side was the free-range herd. Sloan had told her the fence was to keep them in the large pasture where the soil was free of any pesticides or fertilizers.

The wind caught her hair but she barely noticed as she watched the black Angus steers feeding on the tall grass. A calm feeling came over her.

"It's so peaceful here." Although a Texan, she hadn't experienced much of country life.

He sat down beside her and handed her the plastic wrapped sandwich. "Some people would think it's boring." He tipped his hat back and looked out at his herd, with a leisurely gaze. A breeze rustled through the trees. "I call it heaven. That's why I picked this part of the ranch to build a house." He nodded behind him. "It's over there."

"Your house?"

"Don't look so surprised. I haven't lived with my parents since college. I stayed with Mom after her stroke and still do when Alisa and Dad are away. It's only temporary."

Jade rose up on her knees and spotted the buildings off in the distance. "It must be nice to have your own place, yet be close to family."

"It is. The Merricks have been on this land for a long time. They settled in this area around the turn of the last century. Built the first house and barn not far from here." He pointed past the rise. "Started raising Texas beef. And finding oil on your land doesn't hurt, either. Good investments over the years helped out."

Jade was intrigued about the ancestors. Was this her family? "That's quite something to live in the same place for over a hundred years."

He nodded. "The Merricks were even close friends of the Kerry family the town was named for." He gave her an easy grin. "It's said that Angus Kerry beat Otis Merrick in a poker game and got to name the town. If things had turned out differently, it might have been called Merrickville or Merrick Springs."

She caught the glint in his eyes, and reached out and slapped him on the arm. "You're making that up."

"It could have happened that way." He took a big bite of his sandwich and chewed a long time before adding, "But you'll have to ask a true Merrick, Clay or Alisa, about the details."

Jade frowned, unable to finish her sandwich. Would they claim her? "You're part of the family, too, in every way that counts."

He nodded. "And Clay has never made me feel any less, but there are many differences between us. I don't have the drive for political office like he does. And there's pretty much been a Merrick in Washington for the last fifty years."

"I take it you've argued about it?"

He shook his head, but she could see something was bothering him. "Clay's more subtle. But some think because I have the name I should run for office."

"That's crazy."

He looked surprised at her comment. "And I'd make a rotten politician. Alisa would be better at it, but I don't want her to be pressured, either. If you knew my baby sister you'd know that no one can make her do something she doesn't want to do."

"I like her already." Jade might have a half sister. Would she be gone before she got the chance to meet her? "Does she come to the ranch often?"

Sloan opened the cap on a bottle of iced tea. He handed her one. "She doesn't work far away, only in Austin." He took a drink. "She'd like to meet you, too. The woman who helped bring our mother so far along."

"Louisa would have gotten there. She just has a little stubborn streak."

He sobered. "We were so worried about her, especially when she was losing her desire even to do therapy. To us, you're a miracle worker."

"Just doing my job." Would they think that if they knew her real reason for coming here? "Besides, your mother's the one who wanted to improve."

The wind caught the blanket edge and blew it against her leg. That was when she noticed the building clouds.

Sloan looked up, too. "I don't like the looks of this. "We better start back and now."

By the time they'd gathered up their things, and mounted the horses the rain started coming down. Hard.

Sloan knew they couldn't make it back to the house. "We need to find shelter. So we need to pick up the pace a little."

"Okay, I'll do my best," she called to him as the rain penetrated her lightweight jacket and even her blouse.

"So hold on—tight. We're making a run for it." He instructed her to grip the saddle horn, then grabbed Cally's reins. He kicked Amigo's sides and took off over the rise.

Jade gasped, but managed to regain her balance as they cantered across the field. She soon found the rhythm and leaned forward on the horse. It wasn't easy fighting against the wind and rain.

"That's it," he called as he turned toward her. "You're doing great. Just a little farther." They continued through the pasture until they came to an old house.

Sloan jumped off and hurried to help her down. "Go up on the porch while I take care of the horses."

"I'll help." She took Cally's reins and followed him as he led his horse up the one step to the shelter of the porch. She was surprised when Cally obeyed her commands. He tied the animals' reins to the railing.

Just then lightning flashed across the sky, and rain sheeted off the porch roof. "Come on," he told her. "Let's get out of this."

Sloan turned the knob on the front door, but had to push it with his shoulder to get it opened. Brushing away the cobwebs from the doorway, he went in ahead of her. Although the lighting was dim, he could see that the place was worse than he remembered.

Sparsely furnished, the room had a small table with two chairs in the center. Wooden cabinets lined one wall and a chipped sink stood alone in front of the window. A musty smell teased his nostrils. He reached for the light switch, and flicked it on.

"Oh, it's…cozy," Jade said as she followed him inside. She took off her hat and began to wipe the rain from her face.

"There are a lot of words for this place, but that's not one of them."

She shivered. "How about dry?"

"That's a good one. It is dry." He dropped his hat on the kitchen table. "But not very warm." The temperature had dropped suddenly with the storm front. Another streak of lightning flashed.

He walked past the kitchen area into the main living space and the huge stone fireplace. There was wood stacked next to it. "Let's see if I can warm up this place."

He found some matches on the mantel. "I prefer a

gas starter, but I'll have to do it the old-fashioned way."
He spotted a stack of newspapers beside the wood and
used that as kindling. He struck a match to the kindling
and watched as it caught fire. After a few minutes the
flames flared up. He put the screen back.

He glanced at Jade. She was shivering. "Take off
your wet jacket." He went down the hall and yanked a
quilt off a bed. "It's probably pretty dusty but it should
help keep you warm." He wrapped it around her, then
rubbed his hands up and down her arms to help stimu-
late warmth. That wasn't all it was doing.

When she began to sway, he reached out and caught
her. "Whoa, cowgirl."

Jade felt his arms around her waist, holding her
backside against his hard body. Desire shot through
her like wildfire. This wasn't a good idea, but it felt so
good.

"I'm sorry how things turned out," he breathed
against her ear. "This storm caught me off guard."

Jade shivered and not only from the cold. "Just give
me a minute, and I'll be fine," she lied. She doubted
that. The man had kept her off balance since she'd arrived at the ranch.

Finding her footing, she stepped away. "I enjoyed the
ride, even in the rain."

The wood crackled in the fireplace. "Soon you'll be
warm." He placed another log on the grate. "Come sit
down."

She sat on the hearth, feeling the instant warmth. "It
does feel good." She rubbed her hands along the legs of
her pants. "Nothing worse than wet jeans."

"You're right."

Jade sat beside the fire and glanced around the one

story clapboard house. She was more than a little interested in this place. "Who lived here?"

"It once belonged to Otis and Sarah Merrick. It was built in 1905 when they settled here." He looked around. "It's a little neglected now."

"I think it's in great shape."

"Otis built it." Sloan stood and ran his fingers over the rough pine mantel. "Pretty much this entire place. Before he got into the cattle business, he was a carpenter by trade, and he made a lot of the furniture here, too."

She huddled under the blanket. "Tell me more about Otis and Sarah."

"Let's see what I remember. They had four children. Otis Junior, Charles, Samuel and Elizabeth. Charles didn't live past infancy. Otis Junior died when he was a teenager."

Jade shook her head. "How terrible!"

"Life was tough back then. But you're right, that would be awful." Sloan sighed. "There aren't many Merricks left and Clay only had one biological child, Alisa. His brother, Adam, never had children."

Jade didn't know what to say to that. She didn't have real proof that she was Clay's daughter, only words in Kathryn's journal. Of course a DNA test would take care of that.

"Jade?"

She heard her name and looked at Sloan. "What?"

"Are you okay?"

She nodded. "Yes, I'm finally getting warm."

"Good. This fireplace really puts the heat out."

Feeling nervous she looked around the room. There was a lone sofa and an oval braided rug covering the dusty hardwood floors. A sideboard stood against the wall behind a small kitchen table. "A little work and this place could be livable."

He frowned. "I guess it could be. It probably should be maintained better anyway, seing as it's family history." He stood. "Are you warm enough to take a look around?"

"Sure."

He held out his hand to help her up. Jade took it, immediately feeling the warmth of his large, rough palm. That heat he generated quickly spread through her body as he tugged her down a hallway to the largest of the three bedrooms. He flipped on a switch, revealing the space. The focal point was a big bed with a massive carved headboard.

"Oh, Sloan. It's beautiful." She crossed the room and ran her fingertips over the intricate work. "I've never seen anything like this. It's obvious that this took many hours." She glanced over her shoulder. "You're right, this place should be preserved."

Rain pelted the windows as Sloan leaned against the doorjamb. He was surprised at her reaction, her enthusiasm over this house. Her eyes were so expressive, so filled with excitement. How long had it been since he'd seen someone get this much joy out of something so simple?

This woman distracted him, stirred a yearning in him. Damn, he wanted to deny it, tried to tell himself it was because he'd been too long without a woman.

"When was the last time anyone lived here?" she asked.

"From what I understand it hasn't been used since Otis and Sarah passed away. Otis's son, Samuel, married Alice Kerry, the daughter of the town's founder, she didn't want to live in this house. There was a falling out, so her daddy built the house on the hill. Soon after my father, Clayton Samuel, and his younger brother, Adam, were born. Kerry and Merrick merged their land into one large cattle operation and prospered even more. They named it River's End.

"Not long after that Samuel became the town's mayor. A few years later, he ran for state representative, then the senate." Sloan nodded toward the main house. "So from childhood, Clay had been groomed for public service."

"What about Otis and Sarah? Did they ever resolve things with Sam?"

"They never set foot inside the big house, but they lived into their late eighties, only dying a few months apart."

Jade glanced back at the headboard. "It's a shame Otis and Sarah never got to have a relationship with their son."

"But they did," he said. "Although the daughter-in-law wouldn't give them the time of day, Sam came by to see them."

"I'm glad." Sighing, Jade looked around. "I bet with a little cleaning and some paint this place would be almost new again."

"I guess we should preserve our heritage." Sloan looked at the beautiful furniture that Otis had made. "Alisa will inherit all this one day."

He saw Jade stiffen. "It's important to keep it in the family. Didn't your parents have a house?"

She shook her head. "Not anymore. My mother's care was expensive. She had to sell it. My father has never been in my life."

Sloan barely knew Jade, yet he felt bad for her. No

father. "At least you get to keep some of the family's things."

She hesitated. "They don't belong to me, either." Those beautiful eyes were sad as tears filled them. "I'm adopted."

He went to her. "Oh, Jade, that doesn't mean your mother loved you any less."

He leaned closer and closer to her, feeling the heat radiating through her still damp clothes, her scent was intoxicating. His gaze locked on hers with an intensity that seemed hypnotic. He wanted her.

"My mother's cousin, Margaret, asked for most of her grandmother's keepsakes since I'm not a blood relative."

"You are a part of that family, too. Your mother wanted you as her daughter. Did she will those things to you?"

She shrugged. "I didn't want to argue about it. It was a rough time for all of us."

He touched her cheek, telling himself he only wanted to give her comfort. But it was more than comfort; it was need. Her eyes were mesmerizing, drawing him deep into their depths. Silence surrounded them, except for the soft tapping of the rain against the windows.

"You were special to them." He couldn't stop what was going to happen. He leaned down and brushed a kiss across her mouth. When she sucked in a breath, he went back for another taste.

Jade knew she had no business letting Sloan get this close, but she couldn't help herself as she allowed his mouth to capture hers. She couldn't seem to deny him or the desire he stirred in her. When his hands drew her against his body, she was lost.

Her arms circled his neck and she opened her mouth

to deepen the kiss. Sloan was just as eager when his tongue slid inside her mouth to taste her.

Suddenly Sloan's phone rang, bringing her back to reality. She jumped back breaking his hold.

He cursed. "Bad timing. I need to get this." He turned away as he opened his phone. "Hello."

"Sloan, thank God." His mother's voice came over the line. "I've been trying to reach you."

"Mom, what's wrong?" He glanced at Jade, seeing her concern.

"Nothing, I'm fine. It's you and Jade I'm worried about. When I couldn't get you on your phone I was so worried you got caught in the storm."

"It's okay, Mom, we found cover. We're at Otis's place."

He stole a glance at Jade's thoroughly kissed mouth and felt another surge of desire. "We'll be riding back as soon as the weather clears."

"That's just it, honey. You need to stay put because there are severe weather warnings out for the next few hours."

The sound of the rain intensified at the same time he lost the connection. "Damn. The phone died." He glanced out the front window where rain was sheeting off the porch roof.

"Well, it looks like we're going to see how well old Otis built this place."

CHAPTER SIX

OVER the next hour, Jade fretted as the wind howled and rain pounded the old house. The windows rattled under the stress, but held. They'd lost the electricity shortly after Louisa's phone call, but there were candles and the light from the fire. Daylight was quickly fading away. And the storm hadn't shown any signs of dying out.

She rubbed her arms in worry as she stole a glance at Sloan. He was kneeling in front of the hearth adding more wood to ward off the falling temperature.

Her gaze moved over his wide shoulders and broad back then down to his narrow waist. Lower still to the well-washed jeans that stretched over his muscular thighs and tight rear end. He lifted the log with ease, exhibiting the strength of his arms. The memory of being in those arms was very vivid in her mind. The feel and taste of his mouth, his body pressed to hers. A warm shiver rushed down her spine.

She groaned and looked away. She couldn't let herself be attracted to him. There were far too many reasons to count. Besides, cowboys had never been her type, at least not before she met Sloan Merrick.

She never should have gone riding with him today,

and the kiss was even crazier. When he discovered who she was, she'd probably be tossed off the property.

Ever since learning about her adoption, she'd felt lost. All her life she'd thought one thing, only to learn it had been a lie. Nothing could change the love she'd felt for her mother, but she wanted to know about her biological family. What she didn't need was to get involved with Clay Merrick's stepson. So she had to be sure that he knew that.

"How long are you going to ignore me?"

Jade looked at Sloan. "There isn't anything to say."

"You didn't have any trouble talking earlier. Before I kissed you, and you kissed me back."

"And we probably should leave it at that."

"I agree with you there. You're a beautiful woman, Jade, and hard to resist. It's easy to kiss you, the problem is stopping." He crossed the room. "But I'm going to do my damnedest, because I'm not a good bet. And I definitely don't want anything permanent."

Jade saw a flash of pain across his face. She could tell he was guarding himself, and her heart went out to him. "Who was she?"

He glared at her, then finally said, "Believe me, she isn't worth our time."

The rain pounded against the roof. "It looks like we have nothing but time," she told him.

His gaze darkened and she had trouble not reacting.

"I'm a rancher, a cattleman," he said with such conviction, she knew what it meant to him. "It's what I've always wanted to be since the day I came to River's End when my mother married Clay Merrick. Although for some people they feel you need to be something more. And then they set out to try to change you."

"Why would they do that? You've found what you love to do in life."

Sloan wanted to believe Jade's sincerity, but he harbored too much bitterness. "The game is different when your father is a U.S. senator," he began. "There's the prestige and important connections that go along with the title. It draws the good and the bad."

"I take it…this woman was one of the latter."

He nodded. "That about sums it up. Crystal Erickson came to town and singled me out, telling me she wanted to meet me. We went out for a few months, and it didn't work out. End of story."

He wished it had been simple. Sloan shook his head, thinking about what a fool he'd been, remembering after they'd been dating awhile, he'd come home and found Crystal there. She was talking with his father.

Out of sight, Sloan had listened while she planned out his future. Her dream was for Sloan to follow after Clay. She'd even offered to help prep him to take over the seat in congress someday. She even assured the senator that she could convince his son to run for office. Sloan quickly realized that Crystal didn't love him as much as the Merrick name.

Angry more than hurt, he broke it off with Crystal. She wasn't happy and it didn't take her long to get back at him.

"Even though I ended things between us, my family paid the ultimate price with their story and pictures plastered over the tabloids."

"I'm sorry, Sloan."

"There's no need to be." He shrugged. "It's been over a long time." He didn't want to think about his mistakes. He just knew that he wasn't about to have a repeat in the future.

His gaze locked with hers. This woman could make that damn difficult, make him forget every hard lesson he'd learned from the past.

He forced himself to walk to the window, fighting the pull to go back to her and convince her to do more than share a kiss. The rain sheeted off the window as lightning flashed across the sky, drawing a blanket of intimacy around them. He didn't trust himself.

Sloan glanced over his shoulder to see Jade watching him. He had to remind himself of how foolish he'd been when a beautiful woman was involved, and how in the end the Merrick family ended up as headline news.

He also needed to set things straight. "Earlier I shouldn't have taken advantage of this situation." He didn't want to get any closer to her, either. "What happened between us was unprofessional."

She nodded. "I'm to blame, too. I'm your employee."

He frowned. "You're *my mother's* employee."

Those incredible eyes of hers widened. "Close enough."

"We need to get back. Louisa…"

"My mother is fine. And until the storm passes we can't leave here."

As if to emphasize his words, several flashes of lightning shot across the sky, followed by instant crashes of thunder. She jerked involuntarily.

"Whoa, darlin', I won't let anything happen to you."

She stiffened. "I don't need you to play the big, strong cowboy. I can take care of myself."

Sloan raised a hand. "I have no doubt about that."

He couldn't help but wonder about the things she'd gone through these past months. He could see the sadness behind her toughness. Maybe that had been the reason he'd spoken so freely to her. It was something he couldn't let happen again.

"I should check on the horses." Tugging his hat lower on his head, he opened the door and fought the strong wind as he stepped onto the porch.

He went to the railing and placed his hand on Cally's rump and along her flank. "Sorry, girl, it's going to be a while before I can get you home." He'd removed the horses' tack earlier, but he wished they had more protection from the storm than the two blankets he'd found in the cupboard.

He checked Amigo, then studied the still dark clouds in the dim light. He needed to get Jade out of his head. The last thing he wanted was her as an added complication. No, in a few weeks Jade Hamilton would be back in Dallas, and he'd be working hard at River's End.

That was what he needed to concentrate on now. The ranch. Had he lost any of his herd or his crop from this storm? He didn't need to think about a beautiful green-eyed woman, but that was exactly what he was doing.

He wiped the rain from his face, unable to deny the stirring he felt. He just had to figure out a way to stop it.

Nearly two hours later the freak storm had finally moved on, and Bud had arrived at the homestead with his truck and a horse trailer.

Jade had never been so happy to see anyone. After Sloan kissed her, she knew she couldn't give into her attraction for him. For so many reasons. She was thankful that Sloan had disappeared into the bedroom, leaving her alone by the fire until they were rescued by Bud.

The men loaded the animals and she got in the backseat of the truck. On the trip to the ranch house, she was happy not to have to talk as the men were busy discussing storm damage. She hadn't thought about the toll the heavy wind and rain took on crops and animals. She knew now that bad weather was a threat to a rancher's livelihood.

Bud pulled up at the kitchen door and Sloan climbed out of the passenger seat to help her. The sky was clear, the night cool.

She looked up at him, trying to avoid his gaze. "I can manage, thank you," she said and started to walk off.

He reached to stop her. "It's for the best, Jade."

Ignoring his warm touch on her arm, she looked back at the truck. Bud wasn't paying them any attention. She still lowered her voice and agreed. "It's the only way, Sloan, or...I'll have to leave."

His eyes narrowed. "Dammit, Jade, that's the last thing I want. That's the reason I'm going to stay away from you. I don't want you to leave...for my mother's sake."

So it hurt a little that this all seemed so easy for him. "I'm tired. I'm going inside." She climbed the porch steps and was met by two worried looking women, Marta and Louisa.

Louisa grabbed her in a hug as Sloan and Bud drove off. "Thank God, you're okay."

"I'm sorry we worried you."

Louisa made Jade sit down at the table. "Why? You didn't cause the storm. That cold front wasn't even supposed to come this far south." She shook her head. "I hate to think about what could have happened. Thank God, Sloan was there with you." Louisa glanced behind her. "Where is my son?"

Oh, yeah, without Sloan, she might not be confused about everything. "Taking care of the horses."

Marta brought her a cup of steaming cocoa. "What would you like to eat?" she asked.

Jade shook her head. "I'm not really hungry. I just need to get cleaned up and then sleep." She glanced at Louisa. "If you don't mind."

"Of course not," Louisa said. "Why don't you take your shower and Marta will bring a light supper up to your room?"

Jade was too tired to argue. She stood. "Okay and thank you. Good night."

Jade climbed the stairs to her room and began stripping off her damp, dirty clothes inside the connecting bathroom. Once in the stall, she let the hot water erase the chill from her body. Closing her eyes, she suddenly saw Sloan's face. The look in his eyes before he took her mouth in their first unbelievable kiss. She could still feel the imprint of his body against hers, and it caused a different kind of warmth to shoot through her.

Stop thinking about him.

She finished with a quick shampoo, then got out. She used the blow drier on her hair, and pulled on her satin pajamas.

Returning to her room, she heard the knock. Expecting to see Marta, she called, "Come in."

She went to her bed and pulled back the quilt. "Thank you, Marta, for bringing my supper. I guess I was hungrier than I thought." She turned around and stopped talking. It wasn't the housekeeper, but Sloan.

He hadn't cleaned up yet. But dirty jeans and boots didn't curb the attraction she felt for the man. "What are you doing here?"

He combed his hand through his hair as his interest went to her state of dress. "Damn, you even look sexy in pj's."

She refused to act embarrassed. "I was planning on getting some sleep. So could we let this discussion go until another time?"

"I didn't like how we left things."

"I thought we agreed it was the only sensible way."

He didn't look convinced, but he didn't move from the spot and Jade was grateful for that. She was afraid how willing she would be if he touched her. He needed to go.

"Look, Sloan, it isn't a good idea you're here…"

"I know. That's why I came to tell you that I'll be gone in the morning."

He was leaving? "Where?"

"Does it matter? I need to be out of here and away from you."

"I can't drive you out of your house."

"First of all, it's my parents' house. I'm only moving back to my home."

"Okay." So he would still be close by. "You don't need to worry, I'll take care of Louisa."

"I'm going to hold you to that," he said. "But if you need me for anything just call down to the barn."

She swallowed. "Thank you for the ride today. Even with the bad weather I enjoyed it."

She saw something flash in his dark eyes, but wasn't sure what it was. "Yeah, so did I…more than I should." He turned and walked out.

Jade released a long breath. Sloan was gone. She got what she wanted, so why wasn't she happy?

The next morning, it was work as usual. Jade hadn't slept well at all, but she needed to get back into a routine and do her job. And she needed to figure out what she was going to do when she confronted Clay Merrick.

At seven o'clock, she'd been in the workout room with Louisa. They'd gone through the routine of exercises, and then both headed for a shower and were downstairs for breakfast by eight. And there was no sign of Sloan at the table.

"Is Sloan coming?" Louisa asked the housekeeper.

Marta poured coffee. "No, he ate very early. He had his bag packed and said he was moving back to his house. He would see you later."

Louisa frowned. "Just like that? He didn't say anything last night." She glanced at Jade. "I wonder why all the hurry?"

"Maybe it's the roundup?" Jade said, unable to think of anything else, though she knew she was to blame for this. He wanted away from her so badly, that he hurt his mother.

"I know I've been taking up a lot of his free time," Louisa said. "He shouldn't have to look after his mother."

"Oh, Louisa, I don't think Sloan minds at all. He loves you."

Smiling, she nodded. "He needs his own life. A chance for love and a family." The older woman looked pensive. "When I learned you two were going riding yesterday, I was kind of hoping…"

Jade's chest tightened, wishing things could be different, for all of them. "That's a nice thought, Louisa, but I'm not in a place to think about starting a relationship."

"Oh, Jade, you don't pick and choose when you fall in love. There isn't a perfect time, it just happens. And I've seen how Sloan looks at you."

Jade's heart began to race. She didn't want to know how Sloan looked at her. Their attraction couldn't go any further. "It would be better if we didn't pursue anything. I'll be going back to Dallas shortly."

"Maybe you'll find another job right here. Our medical center is small, but they're always looking for good nurses."

She didn't want to argue. "I'll think about it," she said, knowing she couldn't consider it at all.

Louisa smiled. "That's all a mother could ask for."

Early the next evening, Jade went to search for Sloan. She walked along the gravel road, trying to come up with something to say to him. Something that didn't sound lame as her reason for coming to his home. She was playing with fire. He was her weakness, and he could easily sway her resolve. She needed to stay away from him, but she didn't listen to her own common sense, even knowing the man was one big temptation.

She came up the steps to the big wraparound porch. There was an old chain swing at the far end. She smiled, knowing how nice it would be to sit out on warm summer nights with someone special.

She shook away the thought of anything that involved Sloan Merrick. He was off-limits to her. There were too many complications to count. One being the reason she was here. The only reason that mattered right now.

She had supper earlier with Louisa. It was obvious that the empty spot at the table made the woman sad. That meant she had to get things straightened out with Sloan so as not to interrupt Louisa's progress. Try to get things back to before…before they touched, before they kissed.

Jade looked at the front door. Everything inside her

told her to turn around and go back, but she still rang the bell. After hearing "come in" she opened the heavy oak door and went inside.

She was greeted by a large entry with nutmeg-colored hardwood floors. A large great room with a mammoth flat-screen television hung over a stone fireplace. The furniture was overstuffed and leather. The soft sounds of country music came from the speakers overhead. This was a man's room.

Jade walked farther into the house, past a divider to find the open kitchen and dining area. Dark stained cabinets lined the buttery colored walls and the countertops and large center aisle were covered in earth toned granite.

In front of a stainless steel stove was Sloan. He was in a white fitted T-shirt tucked into clean jeans. His feet were bare and his hair still damp from a shower. He turned a thick steak on the stove's center grill, then picked up his beer. The longneck never reached his lips as he turned and saw her.

He froze, then said, "What are you doing here?"

Okay, so he wasn't happy to see her. "I need to talk to you."

"I thought we agreed to stay away from each other."

She tried to hide the hurt. "You chose to banish yourself from the house until the day I leave? There are other people to consider here. So get over yourself, cowboy." When he didn't say anything, she said, "This was a bad idea to come here and try to talk to you."

She started to walk away when she heard him call to her. She didn't stop until she reached the door, when his hand on her arm turned her around to face him.

"Okay. I'm sorry. Why did you stop by?"

"It's your mother."

His concern was obvious. "What's wrong with Mom?"

"Nothing, physically. But since you've avoided the house, have you at least talked with her?"

He released her and she missed his touch.

"Hadn't had the chance," he told her. "Okay, I'll stop by and see her tomorrow."

"That's not the problem. She's worried about being a burden to you."

"Whatever gave her that idea?"

"Your quick departure."

Sloan crossed his arms over his chest. He had to do something to keep from touching this woman again. He'd hoped a few days away from her would change things. Damn, it hadn't and he hated his weakness when it came to her. His jaw tightened causing an ache from his teeth to the top of his head. He needed the distraction.

"I did what I needed to do." He shrugged. "It seemed the best solution for the problem."

"I think the better solution would be to try to get along."

He arched an eyebrow. "Darlin', that was our problem, we get along too well."

Something flashed across her face. Was she remembering the sparks, too? She finally glanced away. "I thought we agreed what happened at Otis's house was a mistake."

She blushed, but before she could answer, a loud alarm sound went off.

With a curse, Sloan ran back into the kitchen and saw the grill with flames shooting high into the hood. He turned off the burner, then covered the fire with a large pan lid. Soon the flames were out, but his meal was charred. "Well, I guess it's soup for supper."

That was when Jade took over. "It's surprising you haven't starved. You clean up the mess, and I'll see what I can throw together for a meal."

He glanced over her in her tailored slacks and pretty bright-blue blouse. "You cook?"

She managed a smile. "Of course. My mother made sure of that."

"I thought career women didn't have the desire to spend time in the kitchen."

She frowned. "Don't judge all women by one."

She opened the refrigerator and stood back to allow him to see the many containers of leftovers. "Looks like Marta doesn't want you to starve, either."

He shrugged. "Someone cares if I eat."

"And here I was feeling sorry for causing you to burn your steak."

He'd been caught off guard seeing her walk into his house. And he was drinking her up, unable to get enough of her.

"What can I say? You're one hell of a distraction, Jade Hamilton."

CHAPTER SEVEN

OVER the next few days, Sloan worked nonstop. There had been no more visits from Jade. The last one had ended with a tour of his house, and her wanting to be friends. And all he had wanted was to carry her upstairs to his big bed. Instead he walked her back to the main house, said good-night to his mother and went back to his place. Alone.

Wasn't that what he really wanted? For her to stay away. Hell, yes! He didn't want to get mixed up with a woman again. Not a woman like Jade Hamilton. She wanted something from him that he was not willing to give. His heart.

That was how he'd been talked into helping break two horses they'd picked up at auction last month. He'd been putting it off with so much to do. Since the roundup was set for the coming weekend, what better time.

Hell, he needed to get his mind on something constructive. Something except Jade Hamilton. Anything was worth trying.

Besides, a couple of the young ranch hands were giving him a bad time about one particular horse, Black Knight. A beautiful, big black stallion he'd purchased hoping to breed some exceptional foals. Except this guy wouldn't get anywhere near any of their brood mares until he learned some manners.

Johnny Reeves had lasted the longest on Knight before getting thrown. Wasn't any better for the others who'd tried. They called Sloan. No matter how much he wanted to decline, he was a big believer in doing the same work as he expected from his hired hands.

"You're next, boss," young Johnny called.

Everyone watched and waited. What the heck? He'd put on a show. He walked over to the nervous stallion, calling himself every kind of crazy.

Jade had come out the back door following Louisa when she heard all the commotion down at the corral. She'd looked toward the area and seen several of the ranch hands sitting along the top of the fence, cheering and applauding as a rider climbed in the saddle. Just as quickly, the man was bucked off.

She'd glanced around for Sloan. She recognized his familiar black hat and his slow, deliberate gait as he appeared in the pen.

"What's going on?" she asked Louisa.

The older woman's eyes narrowed. "Oh, my, looks like they're trying to saddle-break Knight again."

"Again?"

"Let's just say that stallion is a little on the stubborn side." Louisa smiled. "Come on, let's go down and watch."

Jade didn't want to appear too anxious to go, but it was difficult not to. "Sure."

They made their way toward the barn, then veered off to the far side of the corral not wanting to cause any distractions.

That was when Jade got the first look at the next

rider. It was Sloan. She hadn't seen him in more than two days, and she was hungry to get her fill. Dressed in leather chaps and vest, he looked the part of a man in charge. He strolled up to the powerful animal and stroked him. There was a gentleness to his touch she could see even from far away.

Neighing, the horse danced away, but two ranch hands held him steady as Sloan checked the cinch.

"Whoa, fella," he coaxed him back in a low, steady voice. Knight blew out a breath as if saying he didn't trust him.

"That's one beautiful animal," Louisa whispered. "Smart, too. Yet, he is totally worthless unless he can be saddle broke. If anyone can do it Sloan can."

Jade couldn't take her eyes off the man or the animal. Pushing his black hat down on his head, Sloan approached the horse. Reins in hand, he grabbed the saddle horn. Then he raised his booted foot in the stir-rup and climbed on just as the horse swung around in a circle. Gripping the reins, he pulled them back, as the animal reared.

Sloan was ready.

Knight bucked, and then bucked again. Power against power, stubbornness against stubbornness, the dance continued on for what seemed an endless amount of time. Neither willing to give in.

It was incredible to watch.

The horse slowed his assault and Sloan thought he had everything under control. Then suddenly the animal changed directions and started all over again. The guys cheered him on as he concentrated on his job. A few more hard bucks in the saddle and his hat came off, and his teeth felt the jarring, too. How could he ever think this was fun?

"Whoa, fella," Sloan soothed, hoping the horse was finally losing steam. Knight puffed air from his nostrils and bobbed his head, then began to walk.

Again he thought he had everything under control. Then he heard his mother's voice. "Good job, Sloan."

He glanced in her direction and not only saw her but her companion, Jade.

For that split second, he relaxed and that was when the stallion started again with a series of bucks. The last one threw him off and he hit the ground. Hard.

"Sloan…Sloan…"

He felt Jade's hands against his jaw. He turned his face toward her touch, her voice.

"That's it," she coaxed. "Come on, Sloan, open your eyes."

When he did he saw her. Those pretty green eyes staring back at him. "Jade…" He groaned feeling the pain in his back and head.

She smiled. "Good, you know who I am."

"Why wouldn't I?" He groaned again. "What happened?"

"You took a spill off a horse."

He cursed as his memory began to return. He tried to sit up, but Jade placed her hand on his chest.

"Whoa, cowboy. Let me check for broken bones."

Bud appeared overhead. "Yeah, Sloan, let Jade check you out."

It was bad enough he'd gotten bucked off, he wasn't going to let her play touchy feely with him, not in public anyway. "I'm fine." He braced himself on his elbows and then managed to sit up. Seeing the concern on Jade's face stopped him.

He glanced at his foreman. "Bud, tell the guys to get

back to work. Have Johnny cool down Knight and put him in the back corral. I'll deal with him later."

"Right, Sloan." Bud walked toward the crew. "Okay, guys, you heard the boss. It's back to work."

Soon the corral was empty except for Jade. She said, "I still want to check you out."

"I said I'm fine." He got to his knees and paused. His head hurt like the devil.

His mother walked over with the aid of her cane. "Sloan, this is no time to be stubborn—you could be seriously hurt."

He managed to get to his feet. "How many times have I been thrown from a horse? Just give me a minute."

Someone handed him his hat. He placed it on his head, but couldn't seem to take that first step.

This time Jade cursed and slipped her arm around his waist. "Come on, Sloan, let's get you up to the house." Before he could take a step someone else came up on his other side.

He looked down and grinned at the dark-haired beauty. "Hey, what are you doing here?"

His sister smiled back at him. "Looks like someone needs to keep my big brother out of trouble. I guess I'm a little late."

"Your timing was always bad." He glanced at Jade. "Jade Hamilton, meet the other stubborn woman in my life, my kid sister, Alisa Merrick."

Jade froze momentarily. Sister! She quickly recovered the shock and said, "Alisa, it's nice to meet you."

"You, too," the girl said. "I've heard so much about you, I had to come home to see this angel who's helping our mother."

"I'm no angel. Just a nurse."

Alisa was in her mid-twenties, petite in size and height. Her midnight-black hair was pulled back into a ponytail, showing off flawless olive skin and piercing ebony eyes. She looked very much like Louisa. Beautiful.

"I know my mother. No one has been able to get past her stubbornness until you did. And as you can see, that stubbornness runs in the family."

They reached the porch where Marta was holding open the door. Alisa and the housekeeper exchanged some words in Spanish as they brought Sloan inside. They went into the sunroom and to the sofa.

"I need my medical bag." Jade started to leave, but Alisa stopped her.

"I'll get it."

Once Jade told her where it was, she thanked Alisa, then turned back to her patient.

Sloan had removed his hat so she began examining his scalp. She felt him tense, but ignored it. Then she found the lump on the back of his head. He sucked in a breath.

"How many fingers?" She held up two.

"Two."

Alisa returned with her bag. She took out her light and checked his eyes. His pupils were slightly dilated. "You might have a concussion." She continued the exam, checking his heart rate and for any abnormal sound in his lungs. Removing her stethoscope, she stood back. "I think you should be checked out by a doctor."

"So that he can tell me what you just said?"

"I also think you should have your back x-rayed. You came down pretty hard."

She watched as Sloan looked at the three women

standing in front of him. "I don't stand a chance of getting out of this, do I?"

All three of them shook their heads.

An hour later Jade sat in the waiting room of the Kerry Springs Medical Center. The one-story structure was buzzing with activity, but the staff seemed to handle all crises in an efficient manner.

"This is a nice place," she said.

Louisa nodded. "It's state of the art. They only completed it last year and it was badly needed in this area. We used to have to go all the way to San Antonio. Clay helped get some of the funding. I'm happy that it was here for me when I needed immediate care. And now, for my son." She frowned. "Do I have anything to worry about?"

Jade knew the question was about Sloan. "As far as I can tell, no, but let's wait for the results of the X-rays."

Just then the doctor walked into the room and smiled when he saw Louisa. "Louisa, you look wonderful."

They all stood, and Louisa spoke. "Tom, any other day I'd love your charming ways, but all I care about is Sloan."

The handsome middle-aged doctor smiled at Alisa, too. "He's fine. Outside of a slight concussion and some bruises on his backside, he's going to live."

"And his back?" Jade asked.

The doctor looked at her as Louisa made the introductions. "Sorry, Tom. This is Jade Hamilton, my nurse. Jade, this is Dr. Tom Gray."

They shook hands. "Nice to meet you, Doctor."

"And it's a pleasure to meet you, too." He smiled. "I hope you don't mind pulling double duty for the next twenty-four hours with a second patient. Of course, I'd ask for hazard pay, because I doubt Sloan will be an ideal one."

"I think I can handle it," Jade said, but knew she had no business being anywhere near Sloan Merrick.

"We all can handle him," Louisa said and nodded to her daughter. "Can we see him now?"

"Sure. Just down the hall, cubicle four."

Alisa walked slowly alongside Louisa and Jade followed close behind. She was relieved to know Sloan was okay, but she didn't need to be his nurse, either.

Inside she found Sloan sitting on the edge of the bed, shirtless. Okay, she'd seen a lot of men's bare chests, but this guy took her breath away.

"How's your headache?" she asked, trying to hide her reaction.

"How do you think? Pounds like he—heck." He glanced at his mother. "I need to get back to the ranch."

"Slow down, son. You need to do what the doctor says. And that calls for you to rest."

"I'm not supposed to sleep."

"The one thing you can do is stop being a pain," Alisa chimed in. "The doctor's going to come back and give you instructions on what to do. I hope he gives you a shot to improve your disposition."

"If you had the headache I do, you wouldn't be real cheerful, either."

Jade watched the sparring between the siblings. Even arguing, it was evident they loved each other, making her realize again that maybe coming here wasn't a good idea.

She didn't want to be the one to hurt this family.

Dr. Gray came in. "You know the routine, Sloan. No strenuous activities. No medication except what I give

you. And you need to be awakened every few hours."
He turned to Jade. "Think you can keep him in line?"

Jade felt every eye on her. "If I can't I expect I can
call in backup."

"I don't need a nurse," Sloan insisted.

His sister stepped in. "No, you need a keeper."

"Okay, Sloan, I'm releasing you to these beautiful
ladies. Try to behave."

He glared at Jade. "I'll be a model patient, Doc."

It was after midnight, and the house was quiet as Jade
headed down the hall. That was when she saw Alisa
come out of her brother's room.

His sister closed the door and walked toward Jade.
"When I woke him, he growled at me," she whispered.
"His pupils are still the same." She motioned to Jade to
follow her to her bedroom.

The room was painted a blue-green color and was as
big as the one Jade had. There was a wrought-iron bed
frame painted white and the queen-size mattress was
covered with another handmade quilt. No doubt one of
Louisa's creations.

The girl led her to a sitting area in front of a bank of
windows. "Since we're staying up most of the night we
might as well get to know each other." Alisa sat down
in a low back chair and motioned for Jade to take the
other. "Of course, I feel like I already do. Mom has
been singing your praises every time we talked on the
phone."

Jade was glad that Louisa liked her so much. "Your
mother has made my job easy. Believe me she's been
doing all the hard work. She's the one who decided she
wanted to get better."

Alisa curled her bare feet under her. "I know that,

and now you have to handle another stubborn Merrick. How do you put up with it all?"

Jade smiled. "You mostly ignore the grumbling, and do your job."

Alisa laughed. "With my brother, that's all you can do. He's been such a grouch these days."

"And you love him," Jade surmised. "It's obvious you all care about each other. And you're protective."

The pretty girl studied her. "With my dad's line of work, we have to be. It's unbelievable what people will do to get a story. It happened to Sloan, that's what made him leery of outsiders coming to the ranch." Alisa smiled. "I'm still wondering how you got past his suspicions."

Jade knew Sloan had every right to be suspicious of her, too. "Your mother helped," she said, and added, "Your brother told me a little about Crystal."

The raven haired Alisa seemed surprised at that. "She was a piece of work. I never thought of her as Sloan's type." She shrugged. "So I wasn't sad when she was gone, but the whole mess changed my brother. Trust doesn't come easily for him anymore."

Jade wouldn't help that. "I can't blame him, especially when your family is in the public eye so much."

Alisa shrugged. "We've never known anything different. And since I'm seriously considering going into the family business myself, I better get used to it"

Jade was surprised. "Are you talking about politics or ranching?"

Alisa laughed. "I guess they do go hand in hand in this part of Texas, but I'll let my big brother handle the ranching part. I hope to be busy working on Dad's reelection campaign, then I'll see how things go. I need

to get some face time, as they say. And who knows
what will happen."

So, someone in the family wasn't afraid of the spotlight. "So you're considering running for office?"

Alisa flashed those dark eyes. "Anything is possible, but please don't say anything. I need a few more
years to see how things go. And there's the fact that
I'm young, and a little too inexperienced to be taken
seriously. Not yet anyway."

Jade remembered Sloan telling her about the Merrick tradition. "I'm sure your father will be happy about
this."

Sighing, Alisa sat back. "We'll see. I know one
person who won't be. Sloan doesn't like the attention
that comes with a public life."

"But that's his choice," Jade said boldly. "Not
yours."

Alisa smiled. "I knew I liked you."

"I like you, too." And she did, but she also knew
her own news might put a damper on this. "How soon
before your father returns home?"

"In a few days."

Hearing the news, Jade tried to stay relaxed. Things
were happening too quickly. Maybe it would be best
to leave and not say anything at all. Then she wouldn't
disrupt so many lives.

At three o'clock in the morning, Jade stood just inside
Sloan's bedroom. She waited for her eyes to adjust
to the moonlight coming through the window before
making her way to her destination.

Seeing the figure in the large bed, she walked toward
him, and then leaned down. "Sloan." She touched his
shoulder causing him to roll over onto his back, expos-

ing his bare chest. The blanket was twisted at his waist, and she wasn't even going to guess what he wasn't wearing under the covers.

He groaned and blinked open his eyes.

"I need to check your pupils," she said.

He rose up on an elbow and nearly collided with her leaning down. "Make it quick."

She held up her penlight, and found their closeness was unnerving her. As hard as she tried to concentrate on the job, this man distracted her in so many ways. Her hand trembled as she tried to hold the light to his face. She was so close she could feel his warm breath against her cheek. Memories flooded back to the day they'd been caught in the storm.

Sloan took her hand in his. "What's the matter, Jade?" He moved his thumb over her palm. "Do I make you nervous?"

His husky voice was doing things to her. She finished the task and clicked off the light. "No, just tired."

"Then go back to bed." His voice lowered as he moved closer. "I have the alarm set and I can come to your room and wake you up." He kept staring at her. "Dammit, Jade, stop looking at me like that."

Even though it was dangerous to be so close, she couldn't seem to move.

Sloan knew he was playing with fire, but when it came to Jade, he couldn't seem to stop himself. He brushed his lips over hers. When she sucked in a sharp breath, he forgot everything, his headache and aching back, mostly his caution to stay away from her. When she responded willingly he captured her mouth. His need quickly intensified and he deepened the kiss, pushing his tongue into her mouth hungry for the taste of her.

She whimpered and wrapped her arms around his neck and touched her tongue to his. He groaned and pulled her down on top of him.

"This is crazy." He kissed her again and again until his need came pretty close to reaching the boiling point. "But I can't get you out of my head."

"Sloan…" She looked at him. "We shouldn't be doing this."

His hands moved over her back, then down to her bottom, pressing her against him. "Yet, we're here."

She closed her eyes. "Sloan," she breathed.

His mouth took hers again, drinking her in like a starving man. He couldn't get enough. He rolled over, pulling her under him. He looked down at her. "I want you, Jade," he breathed, and then kissed her mouth as his hand moved under her shirt. He touched the bare skin at her waist, then moved upward to cup her breast.

She gasped and suddenly jerked away. "I can't, Sloan," she whispered as she sat up and refastened her clothes.

She knew he was angry and had every right to be. "We seemed to be doing a pretty good job."

"Well, it's a good thing one of us came to our senses." She stood. "See you in a few hours."

"Don't bother," Sloan called to her as she walked out the door. He didn't need her to tie him into knots. No woman would do that to him again. He rolled over and winced at the pain in his head, but it wasn't enough to distract him from the woman who just left him.

CHAPTER EIGHT

JADE had no sooner closed Sloan's door and tried to make her escape when she bumped right into a tall, solid figure in the hall.

"Whoa there, miss," a deep voice said as he gripped her arms to steady her.

Jade glanced up and gasped as she caught sight of the older man. There was no doubt who he was, her father. "Oh, Senator Merrick," she managed to say.

Clay Merrick gave her an easy smile, and her heart pounded in her chest. "Guilty. You must be Nurse Jade Hamilton."

Jade swallowed the sudden dryness in her throat. "Yes...yes, I am. I didn't expect you home. Of course you've come home because of your son." She pointed to the door. "I was just checking on Sloan. He received a slight concussion when he was bucked off his horse today."

She finally stole a glance at his hazel eyes then shut her mouth realizing she was rambling.

"I just flew in tonight. And I appreciate that you're here to take care of him. I know how stubborn he can be about taking help."

"Yes, he is. But I can be pretty tough, too." She couldn't stop looking at him. She saw the lines around his eyes, the creases on either side of his mouth. His hair might be gray, but it was thick and well kept. He looked distinguished, yet he wore the clothes of a rancher.

Clay said something she didn't hear, bringing her out of her reverie.

"Excuse me, did you say something?"

"Would it be all right if I went in to see my son?"

She managed a smile. "I'm sure he'd like that."

He nodded. "I won't stay long. I hope we can visit at a more civilized time. I'd like to hear about Louisa's progress."

"Of course. At your convenience, Senator."

He paused at the door. "Since you're pulling double duty right now, we'll do it at your convenience." He smiled again. "Now get some rest, Miss Hamilton."

"Please, call me, Jade."

"Good night, Jade."

Somehow Jade's legs managed to take her down the hall and into her room. After closing the door, she sagged against it. "I met Clay Merrick. My father."

The unexpected feelings caused a tightness around her heart. She'd never had a male figure in her life. No one to look up to. No one to protect her from bad things. Now, her own flesh and blood was right here. But was he hers?

Insecurity and doubt crept in. Had Clay Merrick known about her all these years? Had he just ignored her, not wanting the complication. Tears she didn't expect began to fall, as she thought the worst.

Maybe he would never want her.

* * *

A few hours later, the sun had come up and Jade was still trying to decide whether to pack her bags and leave the ranch, or go and face the senator.

That was another problem to confront. How could she just blurt out, *"Good morning, Senator. Oh, by the way, I'm your long-lost daughter. Don't worry I'm not going to wreck your home or career."*

She paced back and forth in front of the windows and caught sight of two men walking toward the barn. Looking closer, she figured one to be the senator, the other Sloan. She noticed that he was holding his lower back. How had he managed to get out of bed, and get dressed?

She thought back to last night and being in his arms. His touch. A warm rush went through her, heating her insides. She covered her face with her hands. How had she made such a mess of everything? Why hadn't she approached the senator at his Washington office? Now everything had gotten personal. She'd gotten involved with the family. She glanced again at Sloan as he talked to a few of the ranch hands.

It was worse. Her heart was involved now.

Sloan felt like hell today, but he wasn't going to stay in bed any longer. It was nearly the roundup. He wasn't about to postpone that, either.

"Son, are you sure you're all right? Bud said you took quite a spill yesterday."

"He reports to you now?"

"No, he just told me in passing, as did your mother when I got in last night."

His father always seemed younger than his nearly sixty years. He had an easy smile that all the ladies liked, and the men trusted. The perfect politician. In

Sloan's mind, Clay had been a little neglectful of his wife lately.

"Maybe that's where you should be right now, with Mom. She's been working hard on her recovery. I think she'd appreciate your concern."

Sloan pulled open the barn door and walked inside, but stopped when he heard his father call him.

Clay caught up. "Is there something you're not telling me? Is it your mother's health? Although I met Jade last night, we haven't had a chance to talk yet."

"No, she's fine physically." He placed his hands on his hips. "It would have been nice if you'd been home a little more, though."

Clay straightened as they moved down the center aisle. "I told you why—"

"And I don't believe it. I've seen you fly home for less. Why not for Mom?"

His dad looked frustrated. "Because Louisa hasn't exactly wanted me around, okay? I know the stroke has been difficult, but she's pushed me away whenever I tried to help her."

"So you took the easy way out, and just stayed away."

Clay started to answer. Instead he took off his hat and ran a hand over his hair. "Yeah, I guess I did, but a man can only take so much rejection. Dammit, son, she's moved out of our bedroom."

This was getting a little too uncomfortable for Sloan. "Do I need to tell you what to do about that?"

"No." His dad finally smiled. "Maybe we should change the subject. Okay fill me in on her nurse, Jade Hamilton. I can see she's been working wonders."

This time it was Sloan's turn to look away. "Not much else to tell. She came about two weeks ago and she's gotten Mom to do more than everyone else has."

"She's taking care of you, too."

Sloan shrugged, not wanting to explain it. "Jade was checking on me like the doctor ordered."

His father let it drop. "And did the doctor order you to stay off your feet today?"

"He said to rest. I rested, and now I need to get things done. I have a ranch to run, and a roundup to get ready for."

"I'm sure Bud can handle things for one more day. You should go back to bed. You could get some special treatment from that pretty nurse. It might help improve your disposition."

After lunch, Jade was happy about Louisa's request to drive into town, though she was a little surprised that she wanted to leave the ranch so soon after her husband arrived home.

The ride into town was quiet. Louisa seemed distracted and Jade hoped that a visit with her friends would change that.

They walked into the Blind Stitch and quickly the older woman's demeanor changed. Maybe because these ladies had been friends of Louisa's for years. They'd shared good and bad times. Soon she sat down and the group began to work.

Jenny came up behind Jade. "It's nice to see, isn't it? Old friends together. Most of them grew up here. Louisa came here after marrying the senator, but fit in right away."

"You know about everyone in town." Jade envied

the closeness with everyone. "Did you grow up here, too?"

Jenny smiled. "No, in San Antonio. I came to a quilting retreat a few years back. That's where I met the owner of the shop, Allison Cole Casali. She taught me to quilt. I ended up managing the shop so Allison could be a full-time wife and mother. And I continued to work here because I recently got married to a wonderful guy, Evan Rafferty."

"Matt's brother, Sean's other son."

Jenny nodded. "Of course, Evan is the most handsome."

Jade was quickly discovering how much she liked this little town.

"There are a lot of good people here. Everyone I've met seems nice."

"None better." Jenny smiled. "Hey, you could join my beginner's class. I bet I could get you hooked on quilting."

"I'm not sure..." She looked at the group of ladies, knowing it was a pipe dream to think she could live here. "Besides, my job with Louisa is about to come to an end. She's so healthy and her mobility is improving each day. She really doesn't need me."

"That doesn't mean you can't stay in town," Jenny argued. "You just need another job. And I hear good nurses are in demand."

She would love that, too. But getting her hopes up would be hurtful. "We'll see."

Suddenly the door opened and Jade nearly gasped when Clay Merrick walked into the shop. Removing his hat, he squared his jaw and looked as if he belonged there. He came toward them as if he was on a mission.

"Hi, Jenny," he said.

"Hello, Senator."

He then turned to Jade. "Hello, Jade. I know we haven't had a chance to talk yet, and I'd like to very much. My wife's health is very important to me." He gave her a broad grin. "Maybe you can give me some insight into how you've helped her."

She swallowed trying to find her voice. "Certainly. Whenever you want."

He nodded toward the ladies at the table. "Right now, I'd like to take my wife off to lunch. Do you have any objections?"

Jade shook her head.

"Good." He nodded. "If you'll excuse me, ladies, I've sorely missed my wife these past few weeks. If you don't mind, Jade, I'm taking the town car, but I've arranged a ride for you."

When he walked off, Jade couldn't take her eyes off Clay as he spoke, then reached out a hand to his wife.

From across the room Jade could see Louisa's blush as her husband helped her stand. Moments later, the couple walked out of the shop.

"Oh, my, that's so romantic!" Jenny said, releasing a sigh. "Married all those years and he's still courting her. What a man."

"Yeah, what a man," Jade said, knowing her time here was coming to an end. "I better head back."

"Don't be a stranger," Jenny called as she walked out. Once outside in the warm sun she looked where the town car had been parked and found a truck. Sloan Merrick was leaning against the fender.

Oh, great. She didn't need this today.

He didn't look happy, either. "Seems I'm your ride home."

* * *

On the trip back to the ranch Sloan wasn't sure what to say to Jade. All he knew was he couldn't leave things the way they were between them. Not after last night and her visit to his room…and their problem of keeping their hands off each other.

He drove through the front gate, stopped and shifted into four-wheel drive before he veered off to the side road toward the south.

"Where are we going?" she asked.

"Just a short detour. Since Dad had me take him into town, I'm late for my meeting with a contractor. He's going to do some work on Otis's place."

"Really?"

He saw a spark of enthusiasm. "Why would I lie?"

She glanced away. "I didn't say you would. I'm just surprised that you're working on the place so soon."

He turned off onto a gravel road, and downshifted. He winced as he hit a bump.

"I'll admit the house has been neglected, but now that I've seen the run-down condition, I want to restore it. Do you mind going?"

Her beautiful cat eyes narrowed. "Of course not. My afternoon seems to be free."

"Good, then maybe you also wouldn't mind giving some input. I'm willing to bet you could pick colors better than I would. I'd paint everything white."

"Wait, isn't this something that Alisa would want to do?"

He shook his head. "I tried to feel her out but she didn't seem interested." He drove over the rise and the old house came into view. "Besides, this is your fault."

"Me? What did I do?"

"You were the one who got me thinking about

family roots. What better way than to restore the homestead?"

Jade wasn't sure what to say. Since learning the truth about her biological parents, she'd realized many things. Although her mother showered her with love and attention, the lack of a father in her life had left a large void. But did she belong with the Merricks? Did DNA give her the right to barge into their family? And if the senator didn't want her…

Sloan parked next to another truck and got out. Jade wondered if she should stay put, then Sloan poked his head in the open window. "Hey, come on, I am still disabled here. And this contractor was hard to get. So it's now, or I'll have to wait another six months."

"I still think your sister or mother should be the one to make these decisions."

He opened the door and held out his hand. "I talked to Mom. She thinks it's a great idea, but she's not up to it right now. That's why I could use your help, Jade."

She couldn't say no to this man. "Okay." She climbed out of the cab by herself without his help. The less contact with him the better.

In the bright light of day, Sloan could really see everything: the rotting floorboards, the peeling paint and sagging roof. The place looked even worse.

He sighed. "It's going to take some work."

A man came around the side of the house. "Mr. Merrick," he called.

"Yes, you must be Ben Kennedy."

A man looking to be in his middle forties walked up to them. His company logo, Kennedy Construction, was stitched above his shirt pocket. He shook Sloan's hand. "Yes, it's nice to meet you, too." He turned to Jade. "Mrs. Merrick."

Sloan watched a blush cover her face. "Oh, no, I'm just a family friend," she corrected.

Kennedy quickly changed the subject. "Well, I'd love to get the opportunity to restore this place."

"Well, you come highly recommended, Mr. Kennedy." Sloan turned toward the structure. "So is it worth saving?"

"Of course. The house is well built and solid. I haven't seen the inside, but you definitely need to replace the roof and porch, and of course, paint."

"Not any more than I expected," Sloan said. "I'm happy about that."

They walked up to the porch. Opening the door, he allowed Jade to go first, and then followed after her. He was immediately hit with a rush of memories. That stormy afternoon and evening he'd spent here with her. The warm fire, the sharing of personal things, and then the kiss.

He shook away the memories when he heard his name and the contractor asking about the fireplace.

"It works," he told Kennedy. "We got caught in last week's gully washer and that's how I discovered how run-down the place had gotten over the years."

The contractor smiled. "Did you find any leaks inside?"

Sloan shook his head, not mentioning that had been the last thing on his mind. "Not that we could see."

"Okay, why don't we go room to room and you tell me what you'd like done."

Sloan looked at Jade. "Most importantly, we want to keep the integrity of the house."

She nodded. "Yes, preserve its history."

"I agree," Kennedy assured them. "Anything I have to replace will be identical to what was there."

The contractor walked off down the hall, and the two of them followed. Sloan answered as many questions as possible. Nearly an hour passed before Kennedy had everything he needed to write up a bid. He promised an estimate by morning, and then drove off.

Sloan went back inside to find Jade. She didn't look happy as she spoke. "Why did you make him think that we were making decisions together?"

"We are," he assured her and discovered he wanted her opinion for this place.

"But not the way Mr. Kennedy thinks. We aren't a couple, Sloan." She glared at him. "And you've made it clear there can't be anything between us."

She had him there. "I thought maybe we could get along well enough to do this project." He rested his hands on his hips, as he thought about last night and them tumbling around together on his bed. "But if you'd rather keep this business, I could pay you for your help."

Sloan quickly saw that his words hurt her. "I don't want or need your money, Sloan," she told him.

He raised his hand in defense. "Okay, I was wrong to suggest that. I apologize, but please, Jade, I'm out of my element here. I need you."

She finally looked back at him. "Well, since you asked so nicely, I guess I could help…a little."

No matter how crazy it was, or how much he was opening himself up for hurt, he still wanted Jade in every way that was bad for him.

It was best if he remembered what was at stake here or he'd be in deep trouble. And there wouldn't be anyone to blame but himself.

* * *

Jade knew she couldn't keep living in the Merrick home and avoid Clay forever. Even having supper in her room, she needed to do her job. And early the next morning she ran into the senator coming out of Louisa's bedroom.

He was dressed just like a rancher ready to work. "Well, good morning, Ms. Hamilton." He smiled. "So we finally meet again."

She worked to slow her breathing. "Hello, Senator. I didn't expect... I mean I didn't expect to see you up so early."

His smile widened. "I've always been an early riser, but I'm sure you didn't plan on me coming out of my wife's bedroom."

She glanced over his features to see if she resembled him at all. "That's personal, Senator. It's none of my business."

He laughed and she found herself smiling. "Believe me, Jade, my life has been anything but private. Since you are my wife's nurse, you must have experienced similar depression in stroke victims..." He sighed. "Nothing I did or said reassured her. She didn't want me to see her...shortcomings."

They started walking toward the stairs.

"I love my Louisa, so I let her have her way...for a time. It's been darn lonely, too. So with a lot of persuading, I convinced her to let me move back in and help her through this."

"I'm glad. You being here will help Louisa tremendously," Jade told him. And she wouldn't feel so guilty about leaving.

Clay Merrick grew serious. "I'm grateful that my

wife found you. I marvel at the change in her, and her improvement in such a short time."

They walked into the breakfast room. "Louisa has been working hard. I know she's glad to have you home."

"Not as happy as I am to be here." When Marta arrived, he greeted her in Spanish, and then said in English, "Will you please fix a breakfast tray for Louisa and myself? I'll take it up."

"*Sí, Señor* Clay." After the housekeeper left the room, the senator looked back at Jade. "Please sit down. How do you like your coffee?" He went to the sidebar and poured two cups.

She watched his every move, his strong, sure hands and easy manner. How would he handle knowing about her? Would he even believe her? "Just a little cream."

He returned to the table and set the cup in front of her. "So I hear you're from Dallas."

"Yes. That's where I grew up, but I was born not far from here. Austin."

"Nice town." He took a sip of his coffee. "Louisa told me how you spent the past year taking care of your ill mother."

She nodded. *And I discovered that you are my father,* she added silently.

"I'm sorry for your loss."

"Thank you."

He sat back and studied her a moment. "Somehow, you look familiar to me. Have we ever met before?"

Jade froze. Here was her chance to tell him about Kathryn Lowery, but she shook her head. "You probably meet a lot of people in public life."

He nodded. "I do, but your eyes are so different. There can't be two people—"

"I've been told that," she jumped in, fighting to stay calm.

"Unique. Beautiful. I can see why my son is taken with you."

Embarrassed, she straightened. Had Sloan spoken to him about her? "There is nothing going on be-tween—"

He held up a hand. "My son denies it also. And if there is anything going on, that's your business."

Before Jade could come up with something to say, Marta walked in with the food tray. He stood. "Well, I better get back to Louisa. It was nice talking with you, Jade. One favor, please. Could you give Louisa an hour reprieve this morning?"

Smiling, she nodded. "Tell her I'll meet her in the exercise room at ten."

"Thank you." He walked out and Jade released a long breath, trying to steady her heart rate.

Marta returned with a plate for her. "It's so right for the senator to come home. And with you here to help Louisa, everything will be good."

It was good that Sloan had stopped kissing her, making her want what she couldn't have. That Louisa would get better and the family would be all to-gether again. Soon everything would be perfect. When Jade left.

CHAPTER NINE

IT WAS THE first day of the roundup, but not much had gone right so far. Sloan was short five of his crew and already two calves had gotten tangled in some fencing. Then one of the ranch hands had gotten injured when he took a spill off his horse.

The sound of cows and calves bawling as they made their way across the pasture and toward the pens was music to Sloan's ears.

He loved it all even as he rode drag behind the herd. The hard work usually kept his mind from wandering. This had always been a place where he found solitude. Peace. Yet right now, all he could think about was seeing Jade Hamilton at the end of the trail.

The next hour was spent separating mamas from the babies. When it was finally finished, everyone, crew and neighbors, headed toward the patio to be fed their noon meal before they started the branding.

Evan and Matt Rafferty walked up to him. It hadn't been that long ago that the brothers had worked here. Now they owned a spread along with a vineyard.

"Hey, Sloan," Matt called. "Is your mother's nurse still here?"

"What business is it of yours?"

He raised his hands in defense. "Just making conversation. She's a pretty woman, but if she's taken just give me the word and I'll back off."

"Then back off," he snarled, telling himself he was doing Jade a favor to get Rafferty away from her.

With a nod, Matt walked off to catch his brother in the food line.

Bud showed up. "Funny, I didn't know Jade was spoken for."

"Whether she is or isn't, I'm not going to push her toward a man who is an operator. It's well-known Matt has had a string of women from here to San Antonio."

Bud shrugged. "Jade could probably handle him. But it's nice that you're acting as her protector."

He didn't want to be Jade's anything. He wanted her out of his head, out of his thoughts. As soon as she left here he could erase her from his memory. He'd be too busy to even think of her.

Yeah, too busy. Sloan made his way to the patio and saw the tables lined with food. This was an annual tradition at the ranch. Friends and neighbors showed up to help no matter how big the operation.

That was how things were done in Texas.

Besides, Marta was one of the best cooks around. That fact, along with food dishes the other women brought in, was a big draw.

He grabbed a plate and got in line. He was talking to one of the neighbors and heard laughter. He glanced over to see Jade dishing out food and talking to some of the men.

She was dressed in jeans and a bright pink Western shirt. A white straw cowboy hat was perched on her head, her dark hair was pulled behind her ears. Next to her was Alisa, doing her own share of flirting, too. He had a feeling his baby sister had something to do with Jade's new look.

When Jade smiled at one of the crew, he felt his anger building. Damn. He hated the feelings she stirred up.

Lately, he'd stayed away from the house. Not only to give his parents some time alone, but also so he wouldn't run into Jade. But here she was.

In his world.

He took his plate and scooped up some chicken enchiladas, rice and beans and went over to a far side of the patio in the shade to eat in peace. But he could hear Jade's laughter and he saw the line in front of her was longer than the rest.

He finally gave in and looked at her just in time to catch her smile. It nearly took his breath away and a sudden ache settled in his gut.

"Hey, Sloan," his dad said as he walked up to the table. "What are you doing over here?"

He shrugged. "Taking a break."

The tall man's easy smile faded. "What wrong, son? Is your back bothering you?"

"My back is fine." He took a bite of rice and tried to swallow, finally washing it down with a long drink of iced tea. "I just don't feel like watching the men trip over themselves to get to Jade."

The flicker of a smile appeared on the older man's face. "So again I'm asking, what are you doing over here?"

He glanced away. "I'm not exactly her favorite person. So believe me it's better if I stay away."

Clay pulled out the chair across from him, turned it around and straddled it. "I can understand why you're a little gun-shy." He raised an eyebrow, not mentioning

Crystal by name, but Sloan knew that was who he'd meant.

Clay went on. "I don't know Jade well, but from what I've seen and what your mother has told me, she seems like a nice woman."

Sloan knew Jade was nice. "I'm the one who doesn't want to pursue anything." He recalled the things he'd said to her. "I'm not the commitment type."

His father leaned forward. "Funny, I said something similar when I met your mother."

Sloan was doubtful.

"If you don't believe me ask her. We don't pick and choose when love hits us, son." He pursed his lips. "If it's any consolation, your mother said the day you were bucked off Black Knight, Jade was almost in a panic before you opened your eyes."

Although still reluctant, hope shot through him. Was he ready to take that chance again with someone like Jade?

On the afternoon of the next day the roundup had officially ended. Once the sun went down, the celebration went into full swing and the barbecues smoked with tender Texas beef. Strings of colorful lights circled the patio as friends and neighbors laughed and shared stories of years past. A live band was playing the latest country music and couples crowded the dance floor.

Jade wanted to fit in, even for this one night. Alisa had loaned her a denim skirt and a rose-colored Western blouse, along with a pair of buckskin boots. She even managed to dance the two-step with a few willing men she'd met earlier.

Everyone had accepted her because of the Merricks. Clay and Louisa had been gracious to let her join in with their family. Yet, that didn't make her a Merrick. She doubted anything would. Nothing could change the circumstances of her birth.

She thought about the thirty-year-old picture of Kathryn and Clay. It was tucked away in her bedroom upstairs, but she knew there would be problems if it was ever found. There was so much at stake. Not only to the senator's career, but to rest of the family.

And what about Sloan?

She automatically looked around. There was no doubt in her mind how he'd feel about the news. And she cared too much to hurt him this way. No, she had to leave, as soon as her job ended.

Someone touched her arm and she jumped. She turned to find Sloan. The constant ache inside only intensified at seeing the handsome rancher. He was dressed in a wine-colored shirt that hugged his broad shoulders and black jeans that fit to perfection. His dark eyes bore into hers, leaving her unable to speak.

"Dance with me."

She didn't have the strength to deny him and allowed him to lead her to the floor. A soft ballad began to play as he pulled her into his arms. His hand was pressed against her back, causing her to forget everything except this man as they danced to an old song, "Breathless." That was exactly how she felt with this man.

She shut her eyes, wishing she could close out the rest of the world. If only she were allowed to pursue her feelings for Sloan.

Too late, she'd already fallen for him.

Sloan swayed with the music, holding Jade as close as he dared. He didn't want to do anything to scare her off. Unable to resist, he brushed a kiss next to her ear and whispered, "I've tried, Jade, but I can't stay away."

Sloan heard the catch in her breath, encouraged when she didn't pull away. He danced them to a deserted corner of the patio. Cupping her chin, he kissed her, softly, then deeply. "I never tasted anyone as sweet as you." He pressed his forehead against hers. "I don't know if I can stop."

He could feel her trembling and pulled back to see the desire in her beautiful eyes.

The music ended and a lively song caused the floor to fill up again. He took her by the hand and led her through the crowd, then stopped beside a large tree that shielded them from onlookers. He pulled her back into his arms and bent his head and captured her mouth. The kiss was intense, and feeling her body pressed against his was driving him close to the edge of sanity.

He finally tore his mouth away and said, "Jade, come home with me."

So tempted.

Jade looked at Sloan's outstretched hand. She wanted nothing more than to go with him. But if she spent more time with this man, she'd never be able to leave.

And she *had* to leave.

"Sloan…"

He released a ragged breath. "Don't, Jade. Don't try to tell me you don't want this, too."

Oh, I do, she wanted to scream. He had no idea how badly. She took a step back, trying to break the spell. "Sloan…we've talked about this." She couldn't start anything.

"And it's only gotten us into trouble. We can't seem to stop what's been happening between us anyway. I

can't stay away from you. I can't stop wanting you."
He lowered his head and kissed her. If he was trying to
prove his point, it worked. "Come with me, Jade," he
said as he nibbled along her neck.

She hesitated. How could she? He would hate her
when he learned the truth.

When he released her for a moment, he looked down
at her. "Let's go to my house. I want to make love to
you."

She opened her mouth and he placed his finger
against her lips.

"Look me in the eye and tell me you don't want
me."

She wanted him so much. This one time. This one
night.

When she didn't speak, he took her hand and started
up the gravel road when someone called his name.
Sloan cursed when he spotted Alisa hurrying toward
them. "I'll get rid of her."

His sister was breathing hard by the time she reached
them. She nodded to Jade, then turned to her brother.
"I hate to wreck your evening, but Dad wants us. He's
going to make an announcement."

"Why? This isn't a political rally."

"Sloan," Alisa chided. "It's important, or he wouldn't
ask."

He finally nodded. "Okay. I'll be there in a few minutes."

Alisa smiled at Jade. "I'm sorry." She turned and
walked off.

Sloan took Jade in his arms, pressing his forehead
against hers again. "My dad's timing is rotten."

"It must be important." She felt the tightening in her

chest. "He wants his family all around him for whatever he's going to say."

"And all I want is to be with you." He gripped both of her hands. "Wait for me?"

"It's late, Sloan," she hedged. "Besides, you don't know for sure how long this will take."

"Then let's find out."

She couldn't resist when he tugged on her hand and led her back to the patio. Clay, Louisa and Alisa were already standing on a small stage. The senator was holding the microphone.

Sloan squeezed Jade's hand. "I'll be right back. Promise."

Jade watched as he moved through the crowd and stood beside his sister and mother. Even though Sloan had organized and carried out every detail of the roundup, he let Clay have the spotlight.

"Hey, Jade." Jenny Rafferty came up beside her. "I was looking for you earlier."

"I must have been inside."

The pretty blonde smiled. "Or busy with a certain cowboy." She arched an eyebrow toward the stage. "They're pretty hard to resist. I understand how that is, but I solved the problem by marrying one." Just then a good-looking man came up beside her. "Jade, this is my husband, Evan Rafferty. Evan, this is Jade Hamilton. I'm trying to get her interested in quilting."

They shook hands. "Nice to meet you, Jade. I've heard lots of good things about you from my father and brother."

"Both charming men," Jade added.

Evan tossed her a boyish grin as he draped his arm around his wife. "Just don't believe half of what they say and you'll be fine."

"Stop it, I'm trying to get Jade to stay in town," Jenny said, and then turned back to her. "Kerry Springs is a great place to live."

She would love nothing better. "And when my job ends, I don't have employment."

"If you can't find a position, you could work at the store and there's an apartment above the shop. I used to live there for a while."

Touched, Jade didn't know what to say. They barely knew her.

"Just think about it."

Jade nodded. "Thank you."

The crowd quieted down as Clay began to speak. "First of all, I want to thank my son for putting this roundup together." He turned to Sloan and Jade could see the love between father and son. "You worked damn hard."

Clay turned back to the group. "I also want to thank everyone for coming this weekend, and for all the able bodies who gave of their time and energy. And for those, like myself, who just stood around and shot the bull. We appreciate you coming out, too."

That brought a round of laughs from the crowd. "And, ladies, the food was wonderful as always." He grew serious as he turned to Louisa. "And to my wife." He spoke in Spanish, but Jade understood the words, *Te amo,* my love. He leaned down and kissed her.

"Hey, Clay. You already have our vote."

The crowd laughed as Clay pulled his wife close to his side. "That's the other thing I want to talk to you all about." Again he glanced at Louisa. "We wanted to share our news with friends and family first." He released a long breath. "Although it won't be official until next week," he began, then released a breath. "I won't be seeking another term as your U.S. senator."

A hush went over the crowd as Jade blinked in shock, then her attention went to Sloan. He looked surprised along with Alisa. The only two people who seemed to know what was going on were Clay and Louisa. They seemed rather pleased at that.

When a series of boos began, Clay raised his hand. "Please, don't. I've served nearly thirty years in public life. I'm proud of my record and the job I've done during those years. And Louisa has given up a lot. It's time I give her my undivided attention. While we're still young enough to enjoy life together."

Jade could hear the female sighs in the crowd.

"Thank you all again for coming tonight," the senator said. "Now, let's get this party going."

The music started up as he walked off the stage with his family. The family that didn't include Jade. If not before, she saw it clearly now. She didn't belong here. She thought about Sloan and the mistake she almost made.

She wove her way through the guests and hurried into the house and up the back staircase to the safety of her bedroom. She pulled out her cell phone and called her friend Carrie.

Carrie answered on the second ring. "Jade. Is something wrong?"

"Nothing. Everything. I'll be leaving here tomorrow."

"So you talked with the senator?"

"No. I can't do it." She brushed away a tear. "I realized that I can't cause any problems for his family."

"Jade, you're his family, too."

Her chest ached with longing. This was the part of

her she'd felt missing all her life. She pulled the envelope from the desk drawer. Inside was the treasured photo. "But I can't claim them without possibly destroying everyone in the process." She studied the couple in the picture. "Can I stay with you for a while when I get back to Dallas?"

"Of course, but, Jade, don't leave there until you tell him. For whatever reason Kathryn never told him, you're still his daughter. If you don't, I think you'll regret it."

She couldn't talk about this any longer. "I've got to go. Bye, Carrie."

She shut the phone and studied the picture of Clay Merrick with his staff. Kathryn Lowery stood next to him. While everyone was looking at the camera, she was gazing at Clay. So much love showed in her eyes.

Jade carefully refolded the photo. This was the only picture she had of her parents. And the only other reminder she had was Kathryn's words written in the small journal, telling her about her father.

In reading over the pages, Jade heard Kathryn speak of her love for Clay and the pain she felt at putting her child up for adoption. And Kathryn said that one day, when her daughter was older, she hoped she would want to meet her.

Was that the reason Renee Hamilton never said a word in nearly thirty years about her biological mother? Was she afraid that she would lose Jade? Were Kathryn's words even the truth, or just how she liked to imagine things?

Yet, Jade had to leave it all alone. She refused to make trouble for the Merricks. She'd come to care too much for them. For this town. They'd taken her into their hearts, even Louisa's quilting group had asked her to join them. And there was Jenny's offer... Could this be her home? She had nothing holding her in Dallas.

She glanced down at the picture again. At least she got to meet him. Yet if she stayed, there was always the chance they could discover the connection. It might be a slim chance, but she couldn't continue to live a lie, not with the way she cared about Sloan. He'd end up hating her. She could handle anything but that.

Suddenly a knock sounded on her door and she stuffed the picture back into her purse out of sight.

She went to answer it. "Who is it?"

"Sloan."

She closed her eyes momentarily, trying to gather strength to send him away. She opened the door.

Sloan walked into the sitting area. He held his anger, not only about his dad's surprise announcement, but about the fact that when he needed Jade, she had disappeared.

"I looked for you."

"I thought it was better to let you be with your family."

"You didn't have to disappear. Dad hadn't told us about the retirement until right before he made the announcement."

"You're not happy about his decision?"

"Sure I am, and I'm happy for my mother. She'd love to have her husband around more." He shook his head. "I don't want to talk about my father. Not tonight."

Sloan drew her against him, savoring her softness. He'd wanted this first night together to be at his house, but there was something to be said for spontaneity.

He put his fingers beneath her chin and raised her face to meet his gaze. Then slowly, waiting for her to stop him if she wanted, he lowered his mouth to hers.

Their lips touched, tentatively. She trembled, and he tightened his hold and settled his mouth over hers. When he claimed her mouth the second time, gentleness was forgotten. He went after her like a starved man. He was, for her.

He broke off the kiss. "Don't send me away, Jade."

"I don't want you to go, either," she finally admitted.

Suddenly his throat went dry. He managed to escort Jade inside the dim bedroom. Closing the second door, he pressed her against it, then bent his head and captured her mouth in a kiss hungry with desire.

Slow and easy, that was what he'd planned, but his need was running in overdrive. He pulled back slightly. "Oh, I want you."

She touched his face. "I want you, too. It's just that… your parents are across the hall."

He kissed her, stealing her denial. "Not tonight. They left a while ago. It's only us, Jade. We're all that matters. And you're all I plan to focus on for the next few hours." His mouth took hers in another long, deep kiss that had her swaying into him. "Tell me again you want me."

She breathed out. "I want you again…and again."

He swung her up into his arms and headed for the canopy bed. "I wanted to take you to my bed, at my house, tonight." He laid her down on the mattress and followed after her. "Right this moment, this room seems to be the perfect place because you're here," he breathed against her mouth. "And I promise to show you how special you are to me." He leaned over her, pressing a kiss on each eyelid, then moving down to her nose and then her lips. "How much I care about you."

She touched the side of his jaw and he turned to kiss her palm. "I never felt like this before."

He smiled, feeling the same way. "Isn't that a good thing?"

She wrapped her arms around his neck. "I hope so."

It wasn't long before they were lost in each other. His hands were on the move, caressing her as his kisses got more and more urgent. Then Sloan undressed Jade slowly, his lips trailing over every spot he uncovered, every single inch of her. She did the same for him until he couldn't handle the sweet torment.

He rolled her over onto her back, taking charge once again. As soon as his mouth covered hers, the rest of the world faded away for him.

It was all Jade.

CHAPTER TEN

AT DAWN, Sloan curled into Jade's warmth. He didn't want to leave this bed, or her. He smiled thinking about last night. They'd made love, twice. And he wanted her again, but he knew he had to get up and go to work.

She made a purring sound as she moved toward him, draping her arm over his chest. When she snuggled to get closer he groaned.

"You're looking for trouble, woman," he breathed.

She raised her head, looking surprised he was there. "Oh, Sloan."

"Who were you expecting?"

"No one but you." She gave him a sleepy smile and glanced at the clock, then at the predawn light out the window. "Are you leaving?"

"I don't have a choice, darlin'. The cattle truck is arriving in about an hour to pick up my steers. I need to be there."

He leaned down to give her a quick peck, but it soon deepened into a mind-blowing kiss. He found himself stretching out beside her and their hunger growing to a dangerous level.

"Woman, you are tempting. Could we postpone this a few hours? Meet me at my house later today."

She nodded. "I have to see. I need to do a workout with your mother. When will they be back?"

"Not sure." He knew his parents were off somewhere private. They'd always liked time alone. "I'll call Dad later."

He finally climbed out of bed and pulled on his jeans, followed by his shirt. He didn't miss Jade's gaze on him and he enjoyed her interest. So much so, he had to turn away if he was ever going to leave this room.

"I need to get out of here before Alisa gets up. Clay and Louisa might be away, but my little sis is here, and I'm not crazy about her asking me a bunch of personal questions."

Lying on her side, Jade rested her head on her hand. "Neither am I."

Forgetting the buttons on his shirt, he returned to the bed and sat down. "Do you have regrets?"

She turned those incredible green eyes on him. "No. And I never will."

He leaned down and kissed her. She moaned and her hand began to roam over his chest. He loved her touch. She made him ache.

He tore his mouth away and covered her hand with his. "You've got to stop, or I won't be able to leave."

"You're the one who started it."

"You're right." He stood and walked across the room.

Jade knew she was playing with fire. She'd already fallen for this man. A man she couldn't have. What made it worse was Sloan wouldn't feel the same if he discovered the reason she'd come to River's End.

She needed to get clothes on, too. "Could you hand me my robe?"

"Good idea. You're too distracting," he told her as he grabbed it off the back of the chair.

The fabric caught her purse that was on the arm of the chair and it went flying, dumping the contents on the floor. Jade grabbed the robe from Sloan, slipped it on and went to retrieve the items.

"Sorry," he said.

Jade saw the picture floating to the floor as if in slow motion. "I'll get it." She knelt down, but Sloan was already gathering her things.

He picked up the photo. "What's this?"

Jade tried to snatch the picture away, but he held it out of her reach.

"Some old boyfriend you don't want me to see?"

She shook her head, looking panicked. "No, it's just a picture."

Curiosity and old suspicions got the best of him, and he couldn't resist glancing at the old grainy photograph. There were several people in the scene but the one person who stood out was a younger looking version of his father. A banner on the wall behind them read, Clay Merrick For U.S. Senate.

He turned to Jade, trying to stay calm. "Where did you get this?"

She didn't say anything at first, and then spoke, "I found it."

He started feeling sick. He'd been through this before. "You're here for a story, aren't you? No, don't answer that." He moved away, trying to contain his temper. Past feelings of mistrust surfaced, churning in his gut. He managed to look at her. "Are you even a nurse?"

"Of course I'm a nurse. There was a background check on me. And no, I'm not here to get a story."

"Then tell me where you got this."

She shook her head. "I'd need to talk to your father first."

"The hell you do." His jaw clenched. "You're not getting within ten feet of him, or my mother again. You need to leave. Do you hear me?"

With her nod, he tossed the picture back at her. "One hour, Jade. And you better be gone, or I'll escort you off Merrick land myself."

There was just the echo of the slamming bedroom door as Jade sank down onto the bed. Tears threatened, but she didn't have the luxury or the time to give in to them. She couldn't worry about whether Sloan hated her or not. Nothing she said right now would change that.

She had no choice left but to leave. But with Sloan finding the photo, how could she not tell Clay about their connection. Would he believe her story?

She went to the desk, took out a piece of paper and began to write, telling Clay Merrick her mother was Kathryn Lowery. There could be a chance he didn't even remember her.

This wasn't about her and Sloan anymore. This was about the senator learning the truth about what happened all those years ago. It would be up to Clay if he wanted to know more. He could get in touch with her. She signed her name and found an envelope, stuffed the letter inside and sealed it.

Jade opened her suitcase on the unmade bed trying not to think about when Sloan made love to her, just hours ago. How special he'd made her feel.

She knew he cared about her, too, but because of who she was, she killed those feelings quickly. Although she never lied to him, she hadn't been truthful, either. He would never forgive her for that. She could never forgive herself, either.

Two hours later, Sloan raced back to the corral on Amigo, both sweaty and exhausted from the long, hard ride. He was still angry, and even the miles traveled over Merrick land hadn't erased the memories of Jade's betrayal.

He doubted anything would.

Once inside the corral, he walked his horse to the water trough and climbed off. That was when Bud came out of the barn.

The foreman glanced over Amigo, then Sloan.

"What the hell?" He jammed his fists against his hips. "Since when do you treat an animal like this?"

"I'll take care of him." After Amigo had enough water, Sloan took the reins and started walking his horse.

Bud caught up with them. "Well, you haven't done a very good job so far."

Sloan wasn't in the mood to talk. "I said, I'll make sure he's taken care of." He stopped in the shaded area and tied Amigo to the railing, then began removing the tack.

Bud stood back and watched him. "Does this have anything to do with your daddy's announcement last night?"

"No! I'm actually happy he's dropping out." He pulled off the saddle and swung it up onto the railing, then grabbed a towel and began wiping down the horse. And maybe once and for all, the public wouldn't be interested in them. "That's nice for Mom."

"Are you worried he'll interfere with your plans for the ranch?" Bud asked.

"Dad's more than welcome to try to ride shotgun over us."

The foreman laughed. "That'll be the day."

Sloan knew Bud had been around a long time, and had never been afraid to speak his mind.

"So what's got you so fired up?"

He didn't want to talk about it. "Nothing, I just wanted some time alone."

The foreman eyed Sloan closely, then called for another ranch hand to cool down Amigo.

"I can do it," Sloan argued.

Bud nudged him toward the barn. "From what I've seen so far you can't even take care of yourself, let alone an animal."

They walked inside the barn, then down the aisle toward the foreman's office. Sloan followed the older man inside the small space, knowing he wasn't getting away without explaining himself. Bud sat down at his desk, concern etched on his weathered face.

"Now, tell me what's really going on. Last night you were happy as a speckled pup. You were dancing around the floor with Jade in your arms."

He didn't want to think about last night. "Jade left this morning. I fired her."

"I see. Does Louisa know this? After all, Jade is her nurse."

"I did it to protect Mom. Jade wasn't here for the reasons we thought." He proceeded to tell the foreman what he'd discovered about Jade.

The foreman took off his hat and scratched his head. "Seems to me, maybe you should have given her a chance to explain."

Sloan didn't want to think about her. "If she wasn't guilty why did she refuse to tell me anything?"

"Yeah, son, you got me there. It's not like you to bully a person. Make it so she didn't have a choice but to leave." He shook his head. "No, you'd never let the sins of a past relationship cloud your judgment."

Sloan pushed aside any thoughts that Jade could be innocent. "I'm aware of what people will do to invade our privacy. I need to protect my family."

"Maybe you just needed to protect your own heart."

By the time Jade got into town her tears had dried, but she wasn't sure what to do next. She'd left the note for the senator with Marta. She was told that Clay and Louisa would return home by the afternoon. The housekeeper promised to put the envelope on his desk. It was finally set into motion. Now it was up to Clay Merrick to decide if he wanted to see her. If not, she would be gone and never bother him again. Still she had to wait out the next twenty-four hours.

Jade parked in front of the Blind Stitch. She sat in the car a few minutes, trying to get up enough nerve to go inside. She wanted to touch base with Jenny Rafferty one last time, just in case she had to leave town. She'd been the one person, besides Louisa and Alisa, who she'd begun to strike up a friendship with. She didn't want to go without saying goodbye.

Climbing out of her car, Jade walked into the shop. For a change the place was nearly empty. She spotted Millie with a lone customer.

Jenny came out of the back room. "Jade. What brings you into town today?" the blonde greeted her, then glanced around. "Is Louisa with you?"

"No, it's just me. I wanted to stop by to see you…because I don't know how much longer I'll be in town."

The blonde blinked. "Why? What happened?"

She felt her emotions begin to surface again. "I'm no longer working for the Merricks."

Jenny looked surprised. "Is Louisa well enough to handle her recovery on her own?"

"She'll be fine as long as she continues her exercises."

The blonde regarded Jade for a moment. "I have a feeling this sudden change has more to do with her good-looking son, than with Louisa."

"I was wrong to get involved with Sloan. It was unprofessional."

The bell over the door rang and several customers walked in. Jenny took Jade by the arm. "Come with me."

They walked to the back of the store. She spoke to Millie then led Jade up a back staircase. At the top of the stairs, she found herself in an attic apartment. There was a rather large room that made up a living area and a kitchen.

"This is the apartment I was talking about," Jenny said. "I lived here before I married Evan. Great memories." She sighed. "Enough about me. It's you I'm worried about."

Jade shook her head. "There's no need to worry, Jenny. I'll find another job as soon as I get back to Dallas."

"Dallas? You don't want to go back there, do you?"

Jade looked away. "It's been my home for most of my life." Until she came here, she added silently.

"I know it's none of my business," Jenny began, "but this has man troubles written all over it."

She nodded. "It's more than that."

"Like what? Have you broken any laws?"

"Of course not."

Jenny smiled. "Then stay here and find other employment. And forget about Sloan. He's not the only man in town."

Jade didn't want any other man. "I'm not looking for a man. And believe me, it would be best if I leave town. And I'll be gone by tomorrow." Unless the senator called her. Was that wishful thinking?

"At least you're giving Sloan time to come to his senses."

"He has every right to be upset with me. I wasn't exactly truthful with him."

"You have no idea how much I want to know what this is all about, but I'm not asking. What I am doing is offering you a place to stay. Right here." She waved an arm around the room. "It might be a tad dusty, but there are clean sheets in the cupboard along with plenty of towels."

"Oh, no, Jenny, I can't. What would the owner say about it?"

"Allison Casali." Jenny smiled. "That's right, you haven't met her yet. Well, that will have to wait a few more days. She's in Italy right now with her husband, Alex. They have a ranch outside of town. She'll be back next week. Allison helped me out when I first arrived in town. She gave me a job and this place to live. I'm just returning the favor."

"But you don't know me."

"Yes, I do. I've seen you with Louisa. She's a special lady, and you took the time to help her get back to the living. In my book that makes you a good person."

Jade cared a lot about Louisa. "I don't want her to be

hurt by this, or her family." Tears threatened again. "It was a mistake coming to Kerry Springs."

"Oh, Jade. I wish I could help you, but just so you know, if you ever need to talk, I'm here."

Jade shook her head, wishing she could, but lately trust didn't come easy. "Thank you. But I've made this mess, I need to figure out how to fix it."

"Okay. You rest now. I'll get you something to eat. Maybe that will help you feel better."

Jade nodded, but she doubted anything would help when she knew she'd hurt the family. A family she truly cared about.

Clay and Louisa arrived home by late afternoon. Sloan watched as the obviously happy couple got out of the car. Whatever problems they had seemed to have been resolved during their time together. He envied what his parents had. And it made what he had to tell them even worse. He went into the kitchen and opened the door as his father helped his wife up the last step.

"Hey, son," Clay called out.

He went to them and kissed his mother. "I'm surprised you're back so soon."

"I've scheduled a press conference," the senator said. "I have to work on my speech."

Sloan still had trouble believing his father's decision. "So you really are calling it quits?"

Clay nodded. "It's time, son." He leaned down and kissed Louisa. "Your mother made me realize that there's more to life than politics. I want to be with my family. Speaking of which, maybe you should think about something besides the ranch. You work too hard. Take a vacation."

"I have too much to do right now."

His mother stepped in. "Son, I missed my workout this morning." She looked around. "Where is Jade?"

"That's what I want to talk to you about," he told them, and motioned them inside the house. "Could we go to your office?"

With a nod, Clay led the group down the hall just as Alisa came down the staircase. "Hey, you're home."

"I haven't retired yet," Clay told her. "But once I make my formal announcement, we need to deal with the media. Will you work on my committee?"

"Of course."

"We'll talk later, right now your brother has something he wants to talk to us about."

Alisa beamed. "I bet I know what it is."

Sloan felt his gut tighten. Last night he would have hoped for some good news, too. That died a quick death. "No, you don't."

Clay motioned them into his office. "Whatever it is, why don't we sit down and discuss this?" He called for Marta to bring some coffee, then helped Louisa inside the dark paneled room. A large mahogany desk faced the door, with a row of windows along the back wall, framed by floor to ceiling bookcases.

Once Louisa was settled in a chair, she turned to Sloan. "Okay, son, will you please tell us what happened?"

He looked at his parents. "I had to fire Jade."

Louisa's temper flared. "You had no right to do that, she works for me. Better yet, why would you?"

Sloan moved to the other side of the room. "Jade Hamilton was here under false pretenses. She was after a story. She had a picture of you." He looked back at the senator. "It was an old one from your first campaign."

"Son, a lot of people have photos of me. All you have to do is go to my website and print one."

Sloan would give just about anything for it to be that simple. He wanted Jade to be innocent. "Why would she carry it around in her purse? And when I asked her how she got it, she only said she needed to talk to you before she could tell me anything."

"I know how you ask, big brother," Alisa murmured. "It was probably an interrogation."

Clay sat down on the edge of the desk. Sloan knew he was thinking about Crystal and the trouble she'd caused the family. "Maybe I should have her checked out."

"No, I want to talk to Jade first," his mother insisted. "There has to be an explanation." She turned to her son. "I know you're trying to protect us, Sloan, but there's nothing she can say or do that would hurt us."

Marta arrived with a tray of coffee. She set it down on the table and looked at the senator. "Senator, there's an envelope for you on your desk."

"Thank you, Marta. I'll look at it later."

"Please, I promised *Señorita* Jade I'd make sure you got it first thing."

Clay looked over his shoulder and found the envelope. "Maybe this will answer our questions." He opened the envelope and pulled out the single sheet of stationery. The room was silent as he began to read, then slowly the senator's face paled.

"What does she say, Clay?" Louisa asked.

"She talks about finding her adoption papers in a safe-deposit box of her mother's. She also found a picture of me after I won my first campaign." He looked at his son. "Is that the one you saw?"

With Sloan's nod, Clay read on. "She said there was

also a small journal from her biological mother a... Kathryn Lowery."

The senator turned to his wife and swallowed hard. "How old is Jade?"

Louisa shrugged. "Twenty-nine, I think. Yes, it was on her résumé."

Clay didn't speak for a moment, then said, "Oh, my God, Louisa. I think Jade Hamilton could be my daughter."

Jade didn't have much of an appetite. In fact, she was close to being sick to her stomach. It had all backfired. She only wanted to see where she had come from. To find her biological parents. With Kathryn gone, it was only her father. Now everything was a mess. It was never her intention to hurt this family. She closed her eyes fighting the wave of nausea.

She lay down on the sofa, hoping it would pass. Then she would leave. Tonight. She heard someone come up the steps. Jenny must be checking on her again.

"Did you really think you could get away with it?"

Her eyes shot open and she saw Sloan. "Sloan."

She sat up, then stood. "What are you doing here?"

"You think I wouldn't find you, did you? Well, welcome to small town living. Several people saw you come in here."

Her hungry gaze moved over him. The handsome Sloan Merrick had stolen her heart right from the first. And she had hurt him. Badly.

"I wasn't trying to deceive anyone," she said. "I'm leaving town, so you don't have to worry."

"Then why are you still here? Are you waiting to be paid off?"

That shot went straight to her heart. "No, I don't want

any money. When I came here, I only hoped to meet the senator." She shook her head. "I never expected to be hired that day, I only wanted to see him."

"And he wasn't at the interview," Sloan added.

She shook her head. "Then I thought that if he was coming home soon, I could keep working until that happened." She could see he didn't believe her story. "I'd already decided to leave last night when you came to my room."

"Was I part of the game, too?" He quickly raised his hand. "No, don't tell me. I'll wait until the story comes out to find out how you've rated me as a lover."

She gasped. "Sloan, I'm not selling anything. What I'm telling you is the truth."

He took a step closer. Close enough for her to see the fire in his dark eyes. His jaw was tense. "Excuse me if I don't believe you. I've known people who have done crazy things to get into the Merrick family. The last thing I want is my family name splashed across the tabloids again, so how much will it cost to keep your silence?"

This time her anger got the best of her. "I don't deserve the insults. I'm not Crystal." She clenched her fists to hide their shaking. "If I remember correctly, you were the one who came after me."

"Believe me, it won't happen again. You've killed all trust. And if you care as much as you say, you'll leave town and stay away from my family."

CHAPTER ELEVEN

HER heart breaking, Jade watched as Sloan walked down the apartment steps and out of her life.

Forever.

Trembling she sank to the sofa. She'd never expected to be a Merrick, but hearing the things that Sloan said hurt more than she ever imagined. She only wanted to fit in. Somewhere. It didn't look like Kerry Springs was that place.

She opened her suitcase, gathered the few personal items she'd unpacked, put them inside and zipped the bag. Suddenly her phone rang and she checked the caller ID. Senator Merrick.

Her breath caught. She couldn't answer it. She didn't think she could handle one more rejection. Someone else telling her to leave town.

She went downstairs just as Jenny was closing up the shop. "You're leaving? Tonight?"

"I've decided it's best to go back to Dallas right away."

Jenny nodded. "I'm sorry about Sloan coming upstairs. He convinced me he needed to talk to you. I thought you two were going to make up, but I can tell it didn't go well."

Jade's heart tightened. "It wasn't meant to be. Look, Jenny, I'm sorry about getting you involved in this."

"No, don't worry about it. I just wish I could help you more."

Jade was grateful that Jenny hadn't asked any questions. "I appreciate that and I'll phone you when I get back to Dallas."

"Please do. I mean it, Jade. You have friends here at the shop. So stay in touch."

Would Jenny feel the same way if she learned the truth? Of course her loyalty would go to Louisa.

Louisa. Oh, she was going to miss her. And Marta, and Bud. Tears spilled. Her sister, Alisa.

"I promise, I'll call."

Jenny followed her to the front door, gave her one last hug, then Jade walked outside toward her car. Then she saw the familiar town car, double parked. The back door opened and Clay Merrick stepped out.

She couldn't move.

"Jade, will you come with me? So we can talk."

"I don't think it's a good idea, Senator. I'm sorry that I came here. I never meant to cause you problems."

Main Street was quiet as he walked toward her. A slow smile changed his face. "Now I know why you looked so familiar. You have Kathryn's eyes." His gaze moved over her face. "And her lovely smile."

Her tears spilled over. "You…you remember her?"

"Yes, and if you wouldn't mind," he began and glanced around, "I'd like to talk about this in a little more private setting. Please, come with me."

Still she hesitated. She didn't want to have another confrontation with Sloan.

"How about we go to my office here in town?"

When she finally agreed, Miguel took her bag and

put it in the trunk. She got in the backseat and Clay followed her.

They remained silent until they reached a small storefront in a strip mall on the edge of town. He escorted her through the entrance where there was a small light on in a room in the back. The senator's office.

"I hope you have enough light to find your way. I don't want to draw too much attention to us. Not that I'm ashamed of you, but it's hard for a senator to have any privacy."

Jade's heart was pounding in her chest. "It's fine. I can find my way."

They passed several desks until they reached a private office. That was where she saw Louisa.

Jade stopped suddenly.

"It's all right, Louisa knows everything. She wanted to be here."

Jade went inside. "Louisa."

The older woman didn't say anything at first, then said, "You have a lot of explaining to do, young lady."

"I know." She took the chair that Clay offered. "I can't begin to tell you how sorry I am to have caused so much trouble. Believe me, I never knew any of this until after my mother passed away. Like I said, all the papers were in her safe-deposit box."

Jade reached into her purse, took them out and handed them to Clay. "I tried once to get you at your office, Senator, but your secretary wouldn't let me talk to you unless I said why I was calling. I couldn't do it."

She looked Louisa in the eye. "So I gave up. I really did. Then when I needed to return to the work force, I contacted a nurses' registry and out of nowhere your inquiry came up." She took a breath. "Okay, I was crazy

to send in my résumé. When you called me to come to
an interview, I was shocked." She glanced at the senator. "I told myself that I only needed to see you. But
you weren't there, and I got hired. I'd still convinced
myself that I only wanted to see you, to meet you. And
that would be enough. I wouldn't even have to tell you
who I was."

The room was silent for what seemed to be an eter-
nity as the senator looked over both items, then gave
them to his wife.

"You said in your note that Kathryn died years
ago."

Jade nodded. "From what I gather, she wanted this
to be an open adoption, but died of complications from
pneumonia only a few years after she gave me up. My
adoptive mother was supposed to tell me about her and
give me her things." Jade shook her head. "But for her
own reasons, Renee Hamilton never told me, ever, or
gave me any of Kathryn's things."

After a few minutes, Louisa said, "You look remark-
ably like her." The woman was visibly shaken. "Your
mother was very pretty."

"Thank you."

"Tell me, Jade, why didn't you tell me who you
were?"

"I'd planned to, but after getting to know you all,
I knew I couldn't hurt you with my information." She
looked from Louisa to Clay. "I'm not a child, it's not
like I need a family to belong to. I grew up without a
father in my life." She drew a shaky breath. "I only
wanted a glimpse to satisfy me, to help me fill in the
pieces, except nothing turned out the way I'd hoped."

"You didn't plan on falling in love with my son,"
Louisa said.

Jade hesitated and wanted to deny it, but couldn't. "No, I didn't. I'm sorry. That's all I can say and I'll leave town just as soon as I know one thing." She looked at the senator. "Just tell me, did you care about my mother?"

Clay seemed surprised by the question. He glanced at his wife, then said, "Yes, but we never should have gotten together. I was married at the time."

Jade closed her eyes.

Her father continued. "It's something I'm not proud of, but my first marriage was more or less an arranged union between two political families. I'd been primed for politics from an early age and that included marrying the right woman."

Jade recalled Sloan telling her about the famous Merrick family and how they'd been expected to go into politics.

"Kathryn Lowery was a college student who worked on my first campaign when not many people believed in me," Clay told her. "We had many a late night together during the campaign, and when I won the election, there was a big staff party. When it was over, I took her back to her apartment and we made love."

He swallowed hard. "Suddenly I realized how much I'd come to care about her, but I had to do the right thing. I told Kathryn we couldn't see each other again, then I went home to my wife."

"Did you know she was pregnant with me?"

The senator shook his head. "No! If I had, things would have been different. I would have stood by Kathryn and my child."

Jade brushed away a tear. "Thank you for that." She managed a smile. "Now, I can go back to Dallas with all the blanks filled in." She looked at Louisa. "Again,

I'm sorry, Louisa. If you continue the exercises you'll get stronger every day. Soon you won't even need the cane."

Jade hated that she had to leave, but she forced herself to stand. "If Miguel can take me back to my car, I'd appreciate it."

Clay exchanged a look with his wife. "No, Jade, please, don't leave," he said, looking uncomfortable. "This has been hard for me to take in, but you can't just walk into my life, then walk out. If you are my daughter—and I'm pretty sure you are since your birthday comes exactly nine months after the election." He took a step closer, but didn't touch her. "We've missed a lot of years, Jade, and I'd like a chance to get to know you."

Oh, why did this matter so much to her? She shook her head. "But you already have a family, a son, a daughter. I can't intrude anymore."

Louisa stood. "Yes, you can. When I married Clay twenty-five years ago, I had a son that he accepted without question. And now, I accept you."

A tear hit Jade's cheek, and she wanted so much to feel the happiness, but there was Sloan. He would never accept her. "I appreciate that, but I'm not eight years old, Louisa." She looked at the man who wanted to be a father to her. Her feelings were nearly overwhelming. "And, Clay, you have your career to think about."

He grinned. "I've retired, remember. Besides, over the years, the press has had me fathering numerous children. We've survived many stories." He shrugged. "It happens this time it's true. I'd be proud to call you my daughter, Jade. Speaking of daughters, Alisa is over the moon about this news. You have a sister, Jade."

Jade was thrilled about that, but it was Sloan she was

worried about. "And a stepbrother," she added, recalling how he was willing to pay her to go away. "I can't drive a wedge between you two."

"You won't," Clay assured her. "And as soon as Sloan sees that, he'll come around." He smiled. "So what do you say, Jade, stay awhile. Get to know us. Let us get to know you."

Jade wanted to stay, so badly.

"Of course there's always the chance the media will get wind of this," Clay said. "For now, we have the cover that you're Louisa's nurse."

Jade didn't care about herself, only that she would hurt this family. The last thing she wanted was to destroy Sloan's relationship with his father. "First, we need proof I'm truly your daughter. We need a DNA test."

Sloan looked out the back door waiting for his parents. When he'd returned from his visit with Jade, Marta informed him that Miguel had driven them into town on their own mission.

He had a feeling they went to see Jade, too. Good. The senator would be able to convince her to leave town. Of course there was still a chance Jade Hamilton wouldn't let this go.

If only he could.

He paced as his mind returned to last night when he'd left the barbecue and gone looking for Jade. It was a big mistake going to her room. Yes, he'd been drawn to her from the beginning. He'd never wanted a woman as much as he'd wanted her. Never cared about anyone as much and she'd taken him for a ride. He could never forgive her for that. No matter if he loved her or not.

He froze. Love? No! No, he couldn't be in love with her. Not after her deception.

The car headlights drew his attention and he hurried out to the porch as Clay was getting out of the car. Then he watched his father reach inside to help Louisa.

Sloan went down the stairs. "You're back late. So did you get Jade to leave town…"

"Why would I do that?" his father said.

Sloan looked between his parents. "Surely, Mom, you can't want her here. She's lied to all of us." He looked at his father. "You don't even know for sure that she's your daughter," he went on.

Clay nodded. "We're having a DNA test done."

"Great. And when the tabloids get a hold of it, we're going to be a laughingstock. Again."

"Sloan," his father began. "What is wrong with you? You are talking about my daughter here."

"I thought I was your son."

Clay's gaze softened. "You are my son and that will never change."

Everything inside him hurt. What had happened to his family? "I won't let the media invade my life. I've got to go."

He took off up the road toward his house, feeling his entire world had fallen apart. And he couldn't do a damn thing to stop it.

A few days later, Jade walked into the Kerry Springs Medical Center with Louisa and Clay. Nothing odd about that since she was Louisa's nurse, she told herself.

The senator had already talked to his doctor earlier and had assured Jade that the man would be discreet with the DNA test. Dr. Wills would handle everything personally, and use different names. Suddenly Jade was nervous. She hated to think she might not be Clay's daughter.

As if Clay could see her panic, he took her aside. "Are you feeling okay?"

She shrugged, looking into this man's face, hoping to see some resemblance to him. "What if Kathryn made all this up? I mean there could have been someone else in her life."

"You mean, another man?"

She nodded, feeling more relaxed.

"It may have been thirty years ago, but I remember her and our time together. Maybe I was guilty for taking advantage of her youth and her infatuation with me. There wasn't anyone before me. Our night together was Kathryn's first time," he admitted, his voice low so only the two of them could hear. "And there's the fact that your birthday fits."

She believed his words. He seemed to be happy about Jade being a member of his family, and so was Louisa. And Alisa was excited, too.

Sadness crept in. If only Sloan would change his attitude toward her. She didn't expect his undying love, but at least, maybe they could manage to be civil. She'd given up any notion that Sloan Merrick would ever care for her. For now, she would go for like. Just not hate.

"I don't want anyone to be sorry about my staying in town."

Clay glanced at his wife, then back at her. "No one is sorry. At least, no one who counts."

She couldn't help but think about Sloan. He would always count to her.

* * *

That afternoon, Jade put on a smile and followed Louisa into the Blind Stitch. Her group of friends were at the corner table.

"Louisa, it's about time you got here," Beth said, then sobered. "Lilly said she saw you coming out of the medical center this morning. Is everything okay?"

"Oh my, we can't make a move around this town without someone watching. Yes, I'm fine. Clay's fine, too."

"What about Jade?" Millie asked.

Louisa rolled her eyes, then looked at Jade. "I'm recovering so quickly that I'm not going to need her. But Jade needs a job. What better place than Kerry Springs Medical Center?"

"And especially when she has a senator to put in a good word for her," Liz said.

Louisa's gaze narrowed. "The fact that Jade is a good nurse is word enough. There's always a shortage of those."

The group laughed and Jade found herself relaxing. "Yes, ladies," she admitted. "If you want me to join your group, I need to find work so I can stay and help out with the baby quilts."

Moving to Kerry Springs had a lot to do with Sloan. Could they live together in the same town?

Quickly the topic changed to quilts. This time they were joined by the shop owner, Allison Casali, who had arrived back from Italy that morning. The petite redhead was pretty and friendly.

Allison approached her. "Hello, Jade. I'm Allison Casali. Jenny has told me so much about you."

They shook hands. "It's nice to finally meet you, too, Allison. Your shop is incredible."

"Thank you. Jenny is the one who's put the work into it. Once she started teaching, I thought I was going to lose her, but she was laid off because of school cut-backs. So she still manages the place for me." Allison grew serious. "She told me you might be interested in renting the upstairs apartment."

Jade was interested. "It'll be a few weeks before my job with Louisa ends. Then a lot depends on me finding a new position."

"Not a problem. I didn't plan to rent it to anyone, but Jenny has recommended you highly, so if you decide you need a place, let her know."

"I will. Thank you." Now if only a certain cowboy would be as welcoming.

Liz spoke up. "Hey, let's go and celebrate that we have a new resident in Kerry Springs."

Before Jade could deny anything, the group headed toward the shop entrance. Of course they ended up at their favorite place, Rory's Bar and Grill. Sean Rafferty was there to greet them and give the women his special attention as he led them to a large booth. Jade started to follow the others when someone touched her arm.

She turned to see a smiling Matt Rafferty. "Hi, Jade."

"Matt, hi," she said, not knowing what else to say.

He glanced over her shoulder. "So your boyfriend finally let you out of his sight."

"Boyfriend?"

"At the roundup, Sloan let me know you were spoken for."

How things had changed and so quickly. She shrugged. "That's news to me."

Matt ran his hand over his handsome jaw. "So you're not with Sloan any longer?"

Sadly, she shook her head. "No, I'm not."

"Then how about I give you a call?"

She smiled. It was nice to know that another man found her attractive. Too bad she didn't feel anything at all for this good-looking cowboy. "Matt Rafferty, I hear you have a string of women. Why would I want to be one of them?"

Here came that killer smile of his as he gave her the once-over. "You, Jade Hamilton, could make me give them all up."

She laughed and it felt good, but it quickly died when Sloan appeared at the end of the bar. She wanted to look away, but her gaze was hungry for the man. In his low-riding jeans and Western shirt, he was comfortable in his skin. He was who he was. A rancher.

He was exactly the man Jade wanted.

Matt glanced in the direction that held her interest, then back at her. "Man, I wish you'd look at me like that."

Jade found herself trembling.

"Hey, darlin'," Matt said as he took her hand. "Don't let him see you hurting."

She nodded. "It's not that easy."

"Let me help." His arm went around her shoulders and drew her close, then he dipped his head toward hers and whispered in her ear, "You're too special to put up with someone who doesn't care."

She worked up a smile, then stole a glance at Sloan. He was still glaring at her.

"Let's really make him squirm." Matt kissed her cheek. "How am I doing?"

She opened her eyes in time to see Sloan walk out. "He's gone."

Matt shook his head as he took a look, too. "Merrick is a fool."

"No, he's going through some things. We'll both be fine. I should go, Matt." He reluctantly let go of her hand and she went to the booth.

"Like I said before, Jade," Liz began, "Since you've come to town, you sure have made life interesting around here." She clasped her hands together. "Two men, what a hard choice."

Jade didn't think so, but she couldn't have the one she wanted.

"This isn't a game," Louisa said, then turned to Jade. "Somehow these things work themselves out. But Sloan will need to come to his senses. Knowing my son, that may take a while."

Jade wasn't counting on Sloan at all.

CHAPTER TWELVE

SLOAN had tried to stay busy with work, but since roundup was over, things had quieted down considerably. Although his mother had left several messages, he hadn't felt like talking to his family, not about Jade anyway.

Not since the day he walked into Rory's and saw her there with Rafferty. It hadn't taken her long to find someone else. Why the hell did he care? The last thing he needed was to get involved again with a woman who had another agenda.

He needed to stay busy, so he drove his truck over to Otis's place. The contractor's crew had set straight to work, and already the roof had been replaced along with a new porch floor. The house was painted white with glossy black shutters hung next to the windows.

The place was looking good. So why did Kennedy need him here? Something about inside colors.

There was only one vehicle parked in front. He climbed out of the truck and walked up onto the hardwood porch floor that had been painted a light gray. The front door was partly open. He heard muffled voices coming from the back of the house. He followed the sound down the hall to the third bedroom. The bed was pushed to the center and behind it he saw Kennedy and Jade conferring over paint swatches.

He stopped and drank in his fill of her. She was wearing jeans and a long-sleeve pink T-shirt. The big surprise was seeing buckskin boots on her feet. Her dark hair hung to her shoulders, shielding part of her face. Yet, he'd memorized all her features, her slender nose, full mouth and large green eyes. His breath grew unsteady, but nothing he did stopped his reaction to her.

Then Jade spoke. "I've decided on Needlepoint Navy for the focal wall," she told Ben. "And for the other three walls Summertime Tan."

"Good choices." Ben marked the paint swatches. "The painter will be here tomorrow. Give him two days to finish."

"When do you refinish the floors?" she asked.

"That'll be the last thing we do. I'll check with the plumber to see how he's coming along. You still need new fixtures for the bathroom."

She smiled. "Oh, Ben, they did a wonderful job of reglazing the tub and sink."

"I'm glad you like it." Ben finally noticed Sloan was there. "Mr. Merrick. I didn't see you come in."

Jade looked surprised, too, but not in a good way.

"You were engrossed in your work," Sloan said as he walked into the room. "I see that things are moving along." He stole a glance at Jade. "You've been busy in more ways than one."

"Only doing what you asked me to do," she said.

The contractor looked uncomfortable at the chill between them. "Well, I'll let Jade fill you in," he said, gathering his samples. "I'll call in this order so they can start tomorrow." Ben paused. "Remember, Jade, you'll have to be out for a few days while we do the floors." With her nod, the contractor said goodbye and left them.

Sloan frowned. Jade was living here?

Jade refused to be nervous about Sloan's arrival. She knew that he'd show up sooner or later. She only hoped she'd have other people around.

"Seems you've already moved in, even before the DNA tests are back."

"I still work for your mother, and you asked me to help with this house. I'm only staying here temporarily." And she couldn't sit back and wait for the DNA test to come back. "I'm not going to abandon Louisa because you don't like me."

He didn't look happy.

"I can understand why you're angry, Sloan." She walked up to him. "You ever figure that the reason I couldn't talk to you, or tell the truth was that I knew you'd react this way? You wouldn't have accepted me, no matter what." She blinked, refusing to shed another tear over this man. "Oh, what's the use? You've made up your mind to dislike me."

"That's the problem, Jade. I wish I could dislike you. I wish I could put you out of my mind. All I keep thinking about is being with you. What we shared that night."

He stared down at her and she couldn't stop the tears.

He cursed. "Don't, Jade. Don't cry." He moved in and drew her into his arms.

"I never meant for this to happen," she whispered.

He brushed a tear from her face. He lowered his head and kissed her, softly, sweetly. He drew back and watched her. "Damn, you're so addictive."

Jade wasn't sure what to do. She was afraid to say anything, or do anything to break the spell. So she just enjoyed being in his arms. She'd never dreamed she could ever feel this way, ever care this much for a man. A man she couldn't have.

He brushed his lips over hers again. She sucked in a breath but couldn't manage to release it. She wasn't thinking about anything but being here with Sloan.

Sloan wasn't thinking rationally anymore. He knew the best thing was to let Jade go. Instead he pressed her head against his chest only to feel her softness molded against him. The erratic beating of her heart was in rhythm with his. It would be so easy to get lost in her. Again.

Suddenly something caught his eyes and he saw a shadowy figure move at the window.

"What the hell?" He released her and rushed through the house onto the porch. That was when he saw the guy running to the truck.

"Hey, you! Stop!" Sloan took off after him, then grabbed the back of the man's shirt and pulled him away from the vehicle. Then he turned the man around but didn't recognize him.

"Who the hell are you?"

"I'm Ross Brown. I work for Kennedy Construction. I was coming to do some work and saw you and decided I should leave. Sorry, I didn't mean to interrupt anything."

"It's past quitting time." Sloan tightened his grip, then saw the bulge in the guy's front shirt pocket. Sloan reached in and pulled out a small camera.

"Hey, that's mine."

"Not anymore," Sloan said as he pushed the guy away and began going through the pictures. His anger grew as he saw the photos of him and Jade. "You better start talking, Brown, or I call the sheriff and have him arrest you for trespassing."

The guy raised his hands. "Hey, I've worked on this project. So I'm not trespassing."

"So if I call Ben, he'll tell me he sent you here?" He pulled out his phone. "Last chance."

"Okay, okay. I was at Rory's last night and a guy started talking to me. He found out I'd been working on this job and offered to pay me five hundred dollars if I could get some pictures of any of the Merricks."

Sloan's gut tightened. They were already invading the ranch. Did they know about Jade?

He reached into his jeans pocket and pulled out two one hundred dollar bills and handed them to Ross.

"Here, this is for your camera, and if you show up here again, I guarantee you'll end up in jail."

The guy hesitated only a second before grabbing the money. He walked down the hill toward his truck. After he took off, Sloan called the barn to have one of the ranch hands follow the intruder off their land. Then he dialed Ben Kennedy and told him what happened, and insisted the man not be allowed on the property again. Ben informed him that Ross would no longer be working for him.

Sloan glanced toward the house and saw Jade standing in the doorway. Damn, he hated that this woman could turn him inside out. When the news that she was Clay's daughter got out, it would be a media circus here.

Since their first meeting, she'd been a disruption in his life. She hadn't been truthful, and he couldn't trust her. He hated that even with all the trouble she caused he still cared for her. Far too much.

"I can't do this again." He turned and walked away from her. He hoped for good.

The next day, Sloan had planned a relaxing evening at his house. He'd spent all day repairing fence to avoid everyone. After a shower and a cold beer, his next plan was some supper. He came down the staircase, feeling the cool hardwood against his bare feet. The main floor was mostly open, from the great room all the way back into the kitchen.

He loved this house. When he'd built it, he'd hoped one day he'd have a wife and kids filling the bedrooms. He thought for a second about Crystal and quickly realized she would have never fit into what he'd wanted in a wife, a partner in life. Then there was Jade. He'd thought she was different. In the end, she had her own agenda, too.

There was a knock on the back door and his sister poked her head in. "You busy?"

"You were just in the neighborhood and thought you'd stop by?"

She came in, walked up to the bar and sat down on a high stool. "We live in the same neighborhood. No, I purposely came by to talk to you. Don't look at me like that. If I'd called, you would have made an excuse not to be here."

He went to the refrigerator and pulled out two long-neck bottles of beer, twisted off the tops and handed one to her. "There's a reason for that, sis. I don't want to fight with you, Mom or Dad."

"Then don't drive a deeper wedge by staying away." She hesitated giving him a steady look. "Jade isn't the enemy here."

He took a drink. "Are you saying this is my fault? I didn't lie."

Alisa frowned. "Do you hear yourself? What does Jade have to do with the circumstances of her birth? She didn't break any rules, our father did. Besides, she hasn't said a word to anyone," Alisa argued. "She just didn't tell you her connection to Dad. And me." A slow grin spread across her face. "And you love her."

He glared at his sister. "Go away."

"That's not going to change your feelings for her. I've seen how you two are when you're together. You sizzle." She sighed. "I only wish I'd find someone that made me feel like that."

"It doesn't change the facts."

She snapped her fingers. "Oh, that's right, you're the perfect one. You don't make mistakes, and you're making Jade pay for what Crystal did to you. That's so not fair."

He didn't say anything.

"Here's something to think about, big brother. It's Mom and Dad. They're going to need all of us when this story breaks. And it *will* come out."

Sloan was torn. He knew his mother was strong; she had to be to stay married to a politician. But since her stroke…

"And so will Jade." Alisa set her bottle on the counter and walked toward the door. "By the way, Dad's scheduled a news conference on Wednesday afternoon."

"To officially announce he's not running for reelection?" Sloan said. "Is he also going to announce that Jade's his daughter?"

Alisa shrugged. "The DNA tests are due back by then. It's better to get a jump on the story. That's the reason we all need to be together as a family. Jade is a

Merrick and Dad wants her to be part of this family."
She arched an eyebrow. "Question is, Sloan, are you
going to welcome her, too?"

Wednesday came too soon.

Jade had only seen news conferences on television.
Now, she was part of one. And given the last twenty-
four hours, she wasn't sure she could handle it. Although the DNA tests proved she was Clay Merrick's
daughter, she wasn't sure she wanted to tell the world.
What about the citizens of Kerry Springs? Would they
accept her?

At least the announcement wasn't going to be at the
ranch. It had been a long-standing rule. No media at the
River's End. So Clay was going to hold it at his head-
quarters in town.

She'd made the decision not to go with them. She was
returning to Dallas. For now. Everyone had a lot to think
about. Especially Sloan. Jade could see it hurt them all
that their son refused to be a part of this.

Most of all she didn't want people to think Clay
wasn't running for office again because of her. All the
good work he'd done would be overshadowed by one il-
legitimate daughter.

So the senator's announcement today would be about
his retirement only. And maybe giving Alisa some
needed face time.

Jade's hope was that she could be a small part of the
family. She said her goodbyes and sent the Merricks on
their way.

She could still feel Clay's strong arms around her
and his whispered voice, "I just don't want to lose you,
Jade."

Through raw emotions and aching heart, Jade waved

to them as they drove off. Thanks to her relationship with Louisa, she knew she could come back for a visit without people getting suspicious.

And if her story got out later, they'd deal with it. She wiped at a tear as she thought about Sloan. Maybe at least now he wouldn't despise her.

Bags packed she put them in her car and for one last time she drove away from the special place where she could pretend to be part of this family.

CHAPTER THIRTEEN

SLOAN knew in his heart he couldn't stay away today, so he drove into town. He had to support his father no matter what. He had to stand with his family. After all Clay Merrick had always stood by him. If Clay wanted to claim his daughter, there wasn't anything he could do about it. He would never feel brotherly toward Jade, but if nothing else she deserved to be a Merrick.

Pulling into the parking lot, he saw it was full. There were numerous news vans and reporters anticipating the senator's arrival. But Sloan didn't see his father's town car anywhere when he pulled around to the alley and in at the back of the building. He parked his truck, then went inside the door. Several workers greeted him, but no media people were allowed inside, which he was grateful for.

A few minutes later, his dad appeared along with his mother and Alisa. He combed the area for Jade, but she wasn't with them.

"Sloan, you came," his mother said, surprised.

"I thought you might need me," he told her. "There's quite a crowd out there."

She nodded. "We were expecting this. Your father can handle it."

Clay turned around and nodded. "Glad you're here, son."

Sloan held his breath a moment as his father conversed with one of his workers.

"Where's Jade?"

His father closed the office door, making it only the family. "She didn't come."

"I see that." He looked around at each family member.

"Okay, someone tell me what's going on."

Clay was the first to speak. "I had plans to announce she was my daughter." His father's gaze locked on him. "But Jade said she didn't want to disrupt this family anymore."

Sloan couldn't swallow the dryness in his throat. "She just changed her mind?"

Louisa spoke up. "It was never Jade's idea to announce anything. She only wanted to find her father. Yet, no matter how much we wanted her to be a part of us, she didn't feel as if she belonged here."

Sloan knew why. He was the cause of this. "Okay, I wasn't happy she invaded our lives, but for her to go away?" He suddenly recalled every cruel word he'd said to her and felt ashamed. He had to do something. He headed for the door. "Where is she? I'll go and convince her she belongs here."

"It's too late," Alisa said, looking sad. "She's headed back to Dallas."

Sloan felt like he'd been punched in the gut. "She's gone?"

His sister spoke up. "Does it really matter to you?"

He stared at her. He didn't think she'd leave, not after the DNA results. Truth was, he was the reason

Jade left. In the end it might have cost him his best chance at happiness.

"Sloan."

He looked at his father.

"Are you all right?"

He would laugh if he wasn't so miserable. "Sure, I'm great."

His father gave him a half smile and walked toward him. "If it's any help, I know you were trying to protect us. And Jade knows that, too."

"You were right it could have been handled better. I never even let her have the chance." He looked at the man who'd always been there for him. "I'm sorry. Tell me what to do to fix it."

"This isn't about me, son. I'm going to have a relationship with my daughter no matter if she's here or in Dallas. It's you I'm worried about." Clay leaned against the railing. "Over the years you've had to give up a lot because of me. Your privacy, for one. I know the price you've had to pay, especially with your personal life."

Sloan knew he was talking about Crystal. But in truth, he hadn't wasted much time thinking about the woman in over a year. "Jade is different." Emotions made it hard for Sloan to speak. "I need to make things right."

"I know you do, son," Clay said, folding his arms. "Now, how about you be honest about your feelings for Jade?"

He swallowed, knowing his feelings ran deep. So deep he was not going to let her go. Not if he could help it. "First, if I can get her to forgive me, I plan to stand right next to her, while you tell the world she's a Merrick."

Alisa grinned. "Wow, my brother's in love."

He glared at his sister. "I need to talk to Jade. Dad, can I borrow your plane? I need to get to Dallas."

Clay smiled this time. "There's no need, yet." He checked his watch. "She's probably still at River's End. If you hurry you'll catch her."

Sloan felt excitement rush him. "At the house?"

"No, at her great-grandparents' place. She's saying goodbye."

Sloan recalled all the questions she'd asked about Otis. How much work she'd put into the house. Every detail had to be just right. He felt his chest tighten. What a fool he'd been. How could he think she didn't belong here? He had to get her to forgive him.

Jade stood at the ridge looking over River's End, thinking about the generations of Merricks who'd once lived here. How hard they'd work to build this place, to develop the land. She wished she'd had the chance to learn more about Otis and Sarah. She smiled. Maybe when Clay came for a visit she could find out from him.

She sighed. Staying longer wasn't going to make her departure any easier. Heading back to the house, she took time to examine the simplicity of the new tongue-and-groove flooring that had been painted gray along with the new white railing.

She opened the heavy oak door and walked inside. The scent of fresh paint still lingered as she discovered pretty much everything was finished. The oak floors gleamed a honey hue, the fireplace had been cleaned and Otis's furniture sanded and polished to a high gloss.

The place looked wonderful. She was proud she had been a part in the restoration.

The cozy living room was so inviting. She'd always

felt at home here from the very first. Walking into the kitchen area she could almost picture Sarah preparing supper. She ran her fingertips over the new soapstone countertops. A farmhouse sink was below the window overlooking a corral that had nearly disappeared into the landscape. She bet Otis's wife stood here daily and watched for her husband to come home.

She released a long breath. How simple life had been back then. Just to be able to love someone without any complications.

She knew now that coming to Kerry Springs hadn't been a mistake. She'd found a lot of her heritage, along with her father, and an added bonus, a sister and a wonderful stepmother who'd opened her arms to her.

She always had a home to come to.

Yet, Jade knew she couldn't live at the ranch. It was Sloan's home first, and her being here would only hurt him. She loved him too much to cause any more pain.

Jade continued her journey through the living area and glanced back at the fireplace. This had been where she first started to fall in love with a rancher named Sloan Merrick. Remembering the day they'd been stranded here made her smile, but it didn't stop her tears.

She went into the bedroom. This was her favorite room. It was painted a pretty blue-gray, and the magnificent hand-carved headboard stood out like a piece of art.

Spread across the bed was a beautiful Double Wedding Ring quilt in blues and soft greens. Where had that come from?

She frowned, not expecting to see this here. She raised one of the corners and found the initials QC.

"The ladies from the Quilters' Corner?"

Jade thought about the friends she'd made in town: Liz, Beth, Millie, Lisa, Louisa and, of course, Jenny. No, she had no regrets coming to Kerry Springs.

She had a father. What a lucky girl she was to find him. And as sad as she felt, she was glad she met Sloan, too.

"I'll never be able to come into this room without seeing you."

Jade swung around and saw Sloan. Her breath caught as she looked him over. He was wearing new jeans and a white Western-style shirt. He placed his black Stetson on the dresser and walked toward her. She sucked in a breath, not knowing whether to run or to stay and hold her ground. She just couldn't argue anymore.

"I just came to get the rest of my things." She started for the door. "I'm leaving."

He reached out to stop her, but she stepped away. "Please don't go, Jade."

She paused, trying to gather up enough strength to keep going. "Why? If you're worried that I'll spill my guts to the first newspaper, don't be. I'm not telling a soul that I'm Clay's daughter. Oh, that's right you don't believe anything I say."

He winced. "I was wrong, Jade."

She sighed. "So was I. I was wrong to keep secrets, and wrong to encourage you. What was not a mistake was that I got to meet my father. But don't worry, I'll be gone as soon as I load my car." She glanced away, anything but to look at him. "Goodbye, Sloan. Tell Clay I'll wait for him to call me."

She turned to leave, but this time he stopped her as he took her arm.

"Please, Jade, I know I don't deserve it, but just hear me out."

She shook her head. "I can't do this anymore, Sloan. Isn't it enough for you that I'm leaving town? What more do you want from me?"

"You. I want you, Jade. I know I've made so many mistakes, and I wish I could take all those cruel things I said back. I can't. So I'm asking for your forgiveness, Jade. Forgive me for trying to drive you away. You belong here on Merrick land. And the last thing I want is for you to leave this place."

She could only stare at him, afraid to hope.

"You should be here with your father and sister. River's End is your heritage. Your great-grandfather and grandmother lived here in this house. I understand why you were so interested in the stories when we were stranded here during the storm. You are a Merrick."

"Thank you for that." She blinked back her tears. "I want you to know that I'm not going to take anything from you. I know how important the ranch is to you. That's why I'm returning to Dallas. I don't want you and your family at odds."

"That's exactly what will happen if you do leave."

She paused, searching his face again for any encouragement. He took her hand in his and pulled her closer. She didn't resist as she felt his heat, his strength. Okay, she was weak when it came to this man.

"You can't leave," he continued. "I need you." He swallowed. "I want you to stay not just because of Clay, Louisa and Alisa, but for me, too. You're everything I've ever wanted, Jade."

Her gaze locked with the dark depths of his. She needed more from him. "Why should I stay, Sloan?"

"Because I love you, Jade. I think I fell in love with you the day of the storm, right here in this house. I tried to tell myself it was all physical, that I wanted nothing to do with a woman who needed a commitment. That I could live here, work the land without giving my heart." His hands cupped her face. "Somehow you broke through, and no matter how many times I tried to push you away, I still wanted you. I love you, Jade Hamilton Merrick."

His mouth closed over hers and he wrapped his arms around her, drawing her against him. Her chest tightened with emotion, with longing for this man. He loved her!

The kiss was gentle and tender, and then became intense and hungry. She clung to him, afraid that she would break the spell.

Finally Sloan tore his mouth away. "Jade, when I discovered you were leaving I'd already planned to come after you, to beg you to come back." He looked her in the eye. "I had no business to blame you for what Crystal did. I should have known what a good person you were, just seeing what you've done for Mom." He kissed each eyelid and along her jawline, sending chills down her spine. "Say you'll forgive me, Jade. And please stay."

"Oh, Sloan, I forgive you. I love you, too."

Sloan covered her mouth again and soon they were both lost in the kiss. He didn't mind that, either, except that he had more to do, more to say.

He broke off the kiss and stepped back. "Damn, you're distracting me again."

She laughed. "What did I do?"

"Just looking into those incredible eyes of yours, I get lost." He released her and began to pace the room. "That first day when you arrived at the ranch." He stopped. "No, correction, it was when I saw you in town. Even through my anger, I was thrown by how beautiful you were. I wanted you even then."

She smiled. "You had a funny way of showing it."

"Not anymore." He grew serious again as he stopped in front of her. "I don't want you to doubt my feelings for you ever again." He looked into her wide green eyes and released a breath. "I'll spend the rest of my life proving to you that I deserve your love. I want to share everything with you. I promise that I will always be there for you. Will you marry me, Jade?"

Her eyes widened. "Oh, Sloan. Yes! Yes, I'll marry you."

He suddenly grinned. "Really?"

She nodded and he kissed her.

This time she was the one who pulled back. "I have a question. How will the family feel about us?"

"They've already given their blessing." He pulled her to the bed and raised the corner of the quilt. "As you can see, so have the ladies of the Quilters' Corner."

Jade was surprised. "How could they finish this so fast? We didn't even know."

Sloan shrugged. "I have no idea. Mom says they've been working on it since that day they took you to lunch at Rory's Bar and Grill. Seems when I came in, they could see something going on between us. And they were hoping I would get you to stay."

She touched the beautiful blanket. "Can I ask a favor?"

"Anything. Ask away."

"Do you think we could have this bed? It's so beautiful. I mean, move it to your house." She raised an eyebrow. "That is where we'll be living, isn't it?"

"Unless you don't like the house. I'll build you a new one. Anywhere."

She slid her hands up his chest and around his neck. "First of all, I love your house. I want to live on Merrick land. It's where you run your business." She placed a soft kiss against his mouth. "You are a rancher, and I'll be honored to be a rancher's wife."

"I like the sound of that."

"Maybe we should go and tell the family our news."

"Later." He dipped her toward the inviting bed, but she resisted.

"No, Sloan. That's our wedding quilt and marriage bed. It's for after our wedding."

He groaned. "Then we're going to start a new tradition and have a very short engagement."

Smiling, she went into his arms. "A new Merrick tradition."

He nodded. "Then all I need is enough time to get the bed moved into our house."

EPILOGUE

A MONTH LATER was the big day. Sloan and Jade's wedding day. More had happened over the past thirty days than Jade thought possible, but that was before she had a U.S. senator for a father. Things got done in record time.

She stood in her bedroom at River's End, amazed at her reflection in the mirror. Of all the treasures they had found at Otis's house, this had been the best. In the attic was her great-grandmother Sarah's wedding dress. It needed some repairs and alterations, but the long fitted gown now looked as if it had been made for her.

The ivory satin draped over her slender frame, and then fanned out below the knees creating a long flowing train. She touched the princess neckline with its antique lace insert. The fitted sleeves went from shoulder to wrist and were adorned with tiny covered buttons, ideal for a November evening wedding. The veil was long and had been made for her by the ladies of the Quilers' Corner.

"You look so beautiful," Louisa said, standing next to her in a champagne-colored dress. Alisa was there, too, in a rose hued tea-length gown. She and her younger sister had easily become closer in the past weeks. Alisa was her maid of honor, and Bud was Sloan's best man.

It was hard to hide her excitement. "It did turn out nice, didn't it?"

"More than nice." Alisa whistled softly. "My brother will go crazy when he sees you."

Jade blushed, knowing how anxious Sloan was to get this wedding out of the way, especially since they'd decided to wait until their wedding night before they made love again. Maybe her request was a little extreme, but she wanted the time to get to know not only Sloan but the rest of her family.

There was a knock on the door and Jade quickly called "Come in."

Clay appeared and smiled as he looked her over. Jade had treasured these last days with him, never more than at this moment. He was going to give her away like a real father. He *was* her real father. But it had been Sloan who'd convinced her, then stood by her when Clay announced to the world that she was a Merrick. The citizens of Kerry Springs had been happy with the news.

"You are a vision," her father said as he went to her. "So beautiful." He kissed her cheek as Louisa and Alisa stepped out of the room to give them some privacy. "Your great-grandmother Sarah would have loved you wearing her dress."

She touched the satin. "I feel honored to get the privilege."

"It seems strange that you only just came into my life, now I'm giving you away."

She smiled. "Not so far away. I'll be just down the road. And you'll be seeing us a lot. Besides, with your retirement you and Louisa will probably be gone on vacations."

He grinned. "I'm a lucky guy to have been blessed in so many ways. Not only because you helped Louisa get well, but for the joy you've brought to this family."

"I'm so glad we've found each other, too."

He drew her into his arms. "And no father could be any prouder to have a daughter like you. I love you, Jade Hamilton Merrick." He pulled back, not embarrassed about showing his tears. "Now, it's time I give the bride away. I'm only doing that because I happen to know what a great guy your future husband is. And he will love and cherish you as much as I do."

She blinked trying not to cry, too. She'd come here a few short months ago after learning about her adoption. Not knowing who she was anymore. She not only found a wonderful family, but a wonderful man she loved to distraction.

Music swelled in the background. "That's our cue."

Clay took her by the hand, escorted her out into the hall and down the winding staircase to the main floor. The ceremony was being held in the sunroom with friends and family.

As she walked through the doors, she could smell the scented flowers that had been arranged around the room. Suddenly everyone rose, but she couldn't tell who they were because she didn't see anyone but the man awaiting her at the front of the room.

Sloan looked so handsome in his tuxedo. His thick black hair was recently cut and styled. Her pulse quickened when his smoldering gaze locked on her.

"It's time," Clay said and they started down the aisle.

When they arrived, Sloan met them and the minister asked, "Who gives this woman to this man?"

"Her father and mother do," Clay announced.

Jade glanced at her father, knowing they were both thinking about Kathryn and her difficult decision to give up her baby. Then Clay placed a kiss on her cheek, stepped back and Sloan took his place, his hands warm and strong.

"Hey, beautiful." He winked at her. "What do you say we get married today?"

"I'd love to," she answered him.

They turned to the minister and he directed them through the service. Not that she remembered much. The "I do's" and exchanging of the vows seemed to be a blur. All she saw was Sloan.

The next thing Jade remembered was the minister saying, "I now pronounce you husband and wife. You may kiss your bride."

Sloan didn't need to be asked twice. He leaned down, and covered Jade's mouth with a sweet kiss, controlling his hunger for her. He finally broke it off hearing cheers around the room.

"Te quiero," he whispered for only her. Then he grasped Jade's hand and walked up the aisle as the crowd applauded.

Sloan kept a tight hold on Jade until they reached his dad's study. They went inside and closed the door behind them. He pulled his wife into his arms and kissed her with all his pent-up feelings leading up to this day.

They were finally married.

Jade smiled. "And I love you, too, Mr. Merrick, but if we stay in here people will come looking for us. So we need to get back to the party."

He groaned. "Just so you know we're not going to be the last to leave."

She managed a nod and followed him into the living room where a buffet had been set up.

Jenny came up to them in the receiving line. "It was a lovely ceremony," she told her. "Brings back so many memories of my wedding day. Now, we're expecting a baby."

"Oh, Jenny, I'm so happy for you." Jade hugged her new friend. "Are you feeling okay?"

She nodded. "I'm tired, but good. And Gracie will be a big help to me."

Jade knew Jenny's stepdaughter from seeing the nine-year-old at the quilting class. Now that Jade was a member of the Quilters' Corner, she'd needed some instruction. Louisa had helped, and Jenny had gotten her into a beginner's class. She'd had the chance to meet many more of the women in town. And they all were very accepting of her.

"If there's anything I can do, let me know."

"I'm just happy you're a nurse at the medical center. I hope you're on duty when I deliver."

"I'll try to be there."

Sloan congratulated Evan Rafferty and the couple moved on. The next group was Millie, Liz and Beth.

Finally finished with the greetings, Jade turned to her new husband and smiled. "Oh, Sloan, sometimes I think I'm dreaming." She squeezed his hand. "I've never been so happy."

"That's another family tradition, too. We Merrick men know how to keep our wives happy."

* * *

Sloan thought the reception would never end. Texans were known for celebrating, but it was already after midnight, and that was carrying it too far.

He wanted to have his bride to himself. Although, technically, their honeymoon didn't start until they took off for the Caribbean the next day, late the next day. That was what was nice about having a father who had his own plane. You could make your own flight schedule. And for two weeks, he planned to devote his full attention on loving his bride. Starting tonight.

With the help of his mother, they made their escape out the back door, away from the music and the dozens of people who refused to leave the party.

Jade was just as anxious to go. She grabbed the train of her gown, took his hand and together they made their way to his place.

Correction, their place.

They were a little breathless by the time they reached the front porch. Although Jade had moved most of her clothes in earlier, coming and going across the threshold, he still wanted to follow tradition and carry her into the house where they were going to start their life together.

His two-story house was small in comparison to his parents' but it was plenty big enough for them, and a few kids to boot.

He stopped on the dimly lit porch and turned to face her. "So many times I wanted you here with me. I dreamed of you being here." He blew out a breath. "Now, I'm glad we waited until tonight."

Jade rose up on her toes and placed a soft kiss against his mouth. "I'm glad, too. But now, I'm getting a little anxious, Mr. Merrick. If I remember correctly, you have several fantasies to fulfill tonight."

Grinning, he pushed open the door, scooped her up in his arms and together they entered the house as man and wife. He didn't put her down until he reached the second floor and the master suite.

Jade gasped seeing the bedroom for the first time. The glow of candles lined the edge of the room along with several bouquets of multicolored roses making the area fragrant. The centerpiece was the huge bed her great-grandparents had slept in during their fifty-plus years of marriage. She went to the bed, and touched the carved headboard, then glanced down at the Double Wedding Ring quilt made for her and Sloan.

"This is beautiful." She smiled at her handsome groom, fighting tears of joy. He was still wearing his tux; it was missing his tie and soon she was hoping they would be rid of all their attire. "When did you do all this?"

"I'd like to take credit, but I didn't do it. I have a feeling this was the work of Mom and her friends."

He went to the bottle of chilled champagne in the bucket on the dresser. Once he removed the cap and poured two glasses, he handed one to her. "To many years that we're going to share this bed, and the babies we're going to have."

Jade had trouble swallowing. In the past weeks they'd brushed over the subject, but neither said anything definite. "Babies?"

He nodded, took a drink from his flute, then set down the glass and came to her. "As soon as you're ready, so am I." He took her into his arms. "I want a little girl with your eyes." He placed a kiss on each eyelid. "And your beauty."

"What about boys?" she managed to ask. "I want

them to be strong and good-looking like their father." She wrapped her arms around his neck. "Maybe a little less stubborn."

"Yeah, I'm pretty stubborn, all right."

"One of the many things I love about you, Mr. Merrick. You're fiercely loyal and you love the land."

"And I'm fiercely in love with my wife." He drew her closer. "No more talking, Mrs. Merrick, I only want to feel you, to touch you." He lowered his head and kissed her softly, sweetly. He drew back and watched her. "Damn, I want you so much."

Jade didn't want to break the spell between them as she moved closer. "I want you, too."

Sloan's hands moved over her back. "Dammit, it'll take decades before I can get enough of you. I'll die wanting you." His mouth came down on hers once again.

Jade never dreamed she could feel this way. Never thought she could love any man like this, and now, she knew he felt the same about her.

They'd survived so many hurdles to come to this point. To be able to admit their love for each other. It was something that Kathryn had never been able to do. She couldn't have the man she'd loved so desperately.

He broke off the kiss as he saw her tears.

"Oh, Jade. What's wrong?"

She shook her head. "I was thinking about Kathryn. She loved me enough to have the courage to give me up so I could have a better life."

Sloan brushed away her tears. "All the more reason you should be happy. This was what Kathryn wanted for you. Why she wanted you to have the picture. Now, you have a father."

"You are a good man, Sloan Merrick. And I'm a lucky woman to be married to you."

He smiled. "Okay, how about if I have some of that luck, too?"

As if to prove his point, his mouth covered hers. He angled his head to get better access and deepened the kiss. Making her hungry for more. She would always want more of him.

She had more than luck. She had her man's love and trust. Along with a home and a family.

Oh, yeah, they had it all.

* * * * *

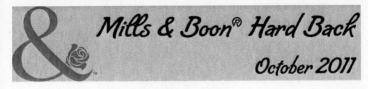

Mills & Boon® Hard Back

October 2011

ROMANCE

The Most Coveted Prize	Penny Jordan
The Costarella Conquest	Emma Darcy
The Night that Changed Everything	Anne McAllister
Craving the Forbidden	India Grey
The Lost Wife	Maggie Cox
Heiress Behind the Headlines	Caitlin Crews
Weight of the Crown	Christina Hollis
Innocent in the Ivory Tower	Lucy Ellis
Flirting With Intent	Kelly Hunter
A Moment on the Lips	Kate Hardy
Her Italian Soldier	Rebecca Winters
The Lonesome Rancher	Patricia Thayer
Nikki and the Lone Wolf	Marion Lennox
Mardie and the City Surgeon	Marion Lennox
Bridesmaid Says, 'I Do!'	Barbara Hannay
The Princess Test	Shirley Jump
Breaking Her No-Dates Rule	Emily Forbes
Waking Up With Dr Off-Limits	Amy Andrews

HISTORICAL

The Lady Forfeits	Carole Mortimer
Valiant Soldier, Beautiful Enemy	Diane Gaston
Winning the War Hero's Heart	Mary Nichols
Hostage Bride	Anne Herries

MEDICAL ROMANCE™

Tempted by Dr Daisy	Caroline Anderson
The Fiancée He Can't Forget	Caroline Anderson
A Cotswold Christmas Bride	Joanna Neil
All She Wants For Christmas	Annie Claydon

Mills & Boon® Large Print

October 2011

ROMANCE

HISTORICAL

MEDICAL ROMANCE™

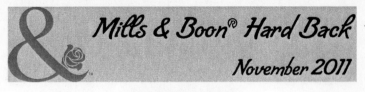

Mills & Boon® Hard Back

November 2011

ROMANCE

The Power of Vasilii	Penny Jordan
The Real Rio D'Aquila	Sandra Marton
A Shameful Consequence	Carol Marinelli
A Dangerous Infatuation	Chantelle Shaw
Kholodov's Last Mistress	Kate Hewitt
His Christmas Acquisition	Cathy Williams
The Argentine's Price	Maisey Yates
Captive but Forbidden	Lynn Raye Harris
On the First Night of Christmas...	Heidi Rice
The Power and the Glory	Kimberly Lang
How a Cowboy Stole Her Heart	Donna Alward
Tall, Dark, Texas Ranger	Patricia Thayer
The Secretary's Secret	Michelle Douglas
Rodeo Daddy	Soraya Lane
The Boy is Back in Town	Nina Harrington
Confessions of a Girl-Next-Door	Jackie Braun
Mistletoe, Midwife...Miracle Baby	Anne Fraser
Dynamite Doc or Christmas Dad?	Marion Lennox

HISTORICAL

The Lady Confesses	Carole Mortimer
The Dangerous Lord Darrington	Sarah Mallory
The Unconventional Maiden	June Francis
Her Battle-Scarred Knight	Meriel Fuller

MEDICAL ROMANCE™

The Child Who Rescued Christmas	Jessica Matthews
Firefighter With A Frozen Heart	Dianne Drake
How to Save a Marriage in a Million	Leonie Knight
Swallowbrook's Winter Bride	Abigail Gordon

Mills & Boon® Large Print
November 2011

ROMANCE

The Marriage Betrayal	Lynne Graham
The Ice Prince	Sandra Marton
Doukakis's Apprentice	Sarah Morgan
Surrender to the Past	Carole Mortimer
Her Outback Commander	Margaret Way
A Kiss to Seal the Deal	Nikki Logan
Baby on the Ranch	Susan Meier
Girl in a Vintage Dress	Nicola Marsh

HISTORICAL

Lady Drusilla's Road to Ruin	Christine Merrill
Glory and the Rake	Deborah Simmons
To Marry a Matchmaker	Michelle Styles
The Mercenary's Bride	Terri Brisbin

MEDICAL ROMANCE™

Her Little Secret	Carol Marinelli
The Doctor's Damsel in Distress	Janice Lynn
The Taming of Dr Alex Draycott	Joanna Neil
The Man Behind the Badge	Sharon Archer
St Piran's: Tiny Miracle Twins	Maggie Kingsley
Maverick in the ER	Jessica Matthews